# Hearts on Fire

## Book One of the Hearts Series

## Sabrina Wagner

# Books by Sabrina Wagner

## Hearts Series

Book 1~ Hearts on Fire (Kyla and Tyler)

Book 2~ Shattered Hearts (Kyla and Tyler)

Book 3~ Reviving my Heart (Kyla and Tyler)

Book 4~ Wild Hearts (Tori and Chris)

Book 5~ Secrets of the Heart (Tori and Chris)


## Forever Inked Novels

Books 1~ Tattooed Hearts: Tattooed Duet #1 (Zack & Rissa)

Book 2~ Tattooed Souls: Tattooed Duet #2 (Zack & Rissa)

Book 3~ Smoke and Mirrors (Draven & Layla)

Book 4~ Regret and Redemption (Chase & Maggie)

Book 5~ Sin and Salvation (Coming Soon!)

# Stay Connected!

**Want to be the first to learn book news, updates and more? Sign up for my Newsletter.**

https://www.subscribepage.com/sabrinawagnernewsletter

**Want to know about my new releases and upcoming sales? Stay connected on:**

Facebook~
https://www.facebook.com/sabrinawagnerauthor

Twitter~
https://twitter.com/SWagnerauthor

Instagram~
https://www.instagram.com/sabrinawagnerauthor

Goodreads~
https://www.goodreads.com/author/show/15944397.Sabrina_Wa gner

**I'd love to hear from you. Visit my website to connect with me.**

www.sabrinawagnerauthor.com

# Table of Contents

# Hearts on Fire

My first love was like fire.
It flickered in the beginning, then blazed to life.
It engulfed my soul and consumed me.
The beauty of the flames blinded me.
I was so entranced by the light and the heat,
That I forgot how easy it was to get burned,
And my heart, incinerated.

# Chapter 1
## Kyla

It was the first day of my senior year at Oak Valley High. I'd spent extra time making myself look just perfect. I added a second coat of mascara to make my green eyes pop and curled my long, blond hair in soft waves down my back. There was only one objective today, and that was to get the football team's new quarterback to notice me. Being the captain of the cheer squad was definitely in my favor. I heard the girls at cheer practice talking about how he had just transferred to Oak Valley from Bay City, which was about two hours north. He was without a doubt the newest attraction at school and I hoped I'd get a chance to meet him today.

I threw on my skinny jeans, a cute pink blouse and my new sandals. I thought I looked pretty. Giving myself one last look in the mirror, I bounced down the stairs and waited for Tori to pick me up. Tori and I had been best friends since the third grade. We were practically inseparable. She was the sister I never had.

When I got to the kitchen, mom and dad were having their morning coffee and looked up when I came in.

"Big day today, sweetie." Dad smiled and held out his arms to give me a hug.

"Yep! I'm so excited to start my senior year," I said moving into his embrace. "This year is totally gonna rock!"

"Well, you look beautiful as always. Do you want some breakfast before your big day?" Mom offered while sipping her coffee.

"No thanks!" I said, as I grabbed a strawberry out of the bowl on the table and popped it in my mouth. "Tori should be here soon to pick me up. We want to get there early to catch up with everybody. Don't forget I have cheer practice after school," I reminded them. Just then I heard the horn honk.

"Gotta go! Love you both!" I blew my parents kisses and grabbed my backpack from the front hallway.

Tori's old, blue beetle was sitting in the driveway, music blaring. I opened the door, threw my stuff in the back and got in. As I looked back at the house, my mom and dad were standing in the doorway, arms around each other, waving good-bye. Tori and I both waved back as she pulled out of the driveway.

"Your parents are so damn cute," Tori said.

"I know it's almost sickening isn't it? They've been together since they were seventeen. I hope I find that someday."

"Kyla, this is our year. We're fuckin' seniors, girlfriend! Time to lose that V card you hold on to so tightly."

"Seriously, Tori? Is that all you think about?"

"Not the only thing. But trust me, Kyla, you have no idea what you're missing! Since Chris and I did it, I can't get enough... of his dick that is!"

"Eww! TMI for sure!" I made a disgusted face. This is what I loved about Tori though. She didn't hold back. I'm pretty sure there was no filter between her brain and her mouth. "I'm not going to have sex, just to do it. It's got to be right. I want it to be with someone I love. I want it all! I want the butterflies in my stomach, the stars in my eyes, the head over heels kind of love. It's out there somewhere." I sighed.

"You're just a hopeless romantic. And I love you for it, but let's be real. The chances of you finding that here are pretty slim. There are no knights in shining armor or white horses, for that matter. Just a bunch of horny teenage boys in pick-up trucks. Not that that's a bad thing." Tori smirked. "Pick-ups usually have bench seats." She waggled her eyebrows at me.

Well, I guess she had a point there.

4

Although we had been friends forever, Tori and I couldn't be more different. She went for the bad boys and had a style all her own. Edgy and carefree. Raven-haired and beautiful.

I was more the classic, All-American girl next door. I was popular because I was nice to everyone. But I'd always played it safe and been the good girl. Sensible, excellent grades, followed the rules...in other words...I'd been friend–zoned too many times to count. Most guys weren't attracted to the good girl. Sure, they were all about being my friend, but boyfriend? That was a different story. They wanted someone willing to stretch and bend the rules.

It's not that I hadn't *ever* had boyfriends. I had. I'd been kissed plenty of times, but none of them had sparked that extra something inside me. I'd always ended up with someone in the "safe" zone. Either they would get bored with me or me with them. Honestly, I couldn't justify wasting time in a relationship I knew wasn't going anywhere. What was the point?

I needed a little excitement in my life but was too afraid to look for it.

I turned to Tori. "So, what do you know about the new guy? He's playing football with Chris, right? Have you met him?"

"No, I haven't met him and yes, he's playing football. I don't really know much about him at all, except he's supposed to be some superstar quarterback." Tori rolled her eyes. "Chris seems to think he's cool though. I think he and Chris drove to school together today, so I guess we'll find out."

"Are you serious?" I panicked. I pulled the visor down and unfolded the mirror. Pulling a tube of lip gloss from my purse, I applied a fresh coat and checked my make-up one last time before we pulled into the parking lot.

Tori started laughing. "What the fuck, girl? He's a football player, not exactly your type. What's with all the primping?"

I sighed, snapping the mirror back into place. "Okay. Here's the deal. I heard he's hot. Like really, really hot. And what do you mean he's not my type? Do I have a type?"

"Uhhh...yeah. You definitely have a type. All the guys you've dated have been the smart, quiet, shy type. I mean they're cute, but in a wholesome way. You know, kind of like a puppy." She laughed at my expense.

I threw up my hands in exasperation. "What? Puppies are cute and loveable."

"Girl, you need a Rottweiler, not a Labrador Retriever." She laughed. "In all seriousness, Kyla, you need to let go a little. You spend so much time studying and trying to make your parents happy. I just want to see you have some fun. Please, just try. Be a little bad, break some rules. You're too damn nice!"

"Number one," I held up my first finger, "there's nothing wrong with nice. And number two," I sighed, holding up the second finger, "you're totally right." I slumped back against the seat. "I just don't know if I have it in me."

We pulled into our parking spot and Tori killed the engine. She turned to me and took my hands in hers. "Listen, you're beautiful, smart, and...I don't mean this in a lesbian kind of way, because I like guys way too much...you're sexy. Own it. Be open to possibilities. Expand your horizons."

"I'll try," I promised. "What do you think is between a Labrador and a Rottweiler, because I'm not sure if I'm ready for that?"

"I don't know. A Labraweiler?" She shrugged.

"That's not even a real thing. Is it?"

"Maybe not, but it might be just what you need."

# Chapter 2
## Tyler

Changing to a different high school senior year fucking sucked! No other way to put it. I'd left all my friends and my team back in Bay City.

My only saving grace was football. Even that wasn't great. Walking onto the team as the starting quarterback, didn't exactly make me Mr. Popular at Oak Valley High. Some guys had been waiting for that opportunity for years, and I just waltzed in and took it. Not that I didn't deserve it. I'd had scouts looking at me since freshman year. Football was the one thing I was really good at.

They'd be changing their tune when I took them to the state championships, which is just what I intended on doing. I got good grades, but football was my thing. I had a natural talent that just couldn't be learned. You either had it or you didn't. That's what my dad always told me. And I had it. I planned on attending either Michigan State University or University of Michigan to play football, although I expected offers from other Big Ten schools as well.

Standing outside the school on the first day, my anxiety was getting the best of me. Chris was hanging with me, while we waited for his girlfriend. At least one guy on the team was cool with me, so I didn't have to look like a total loser.

"Dude, quit fidgeting. You look like a junkie waiting for your next fix." Chris laughed.

"Glad you're finding humor in this. This sucks. New school, new friends, new team." I sighed. "I just want this day over!"

"Be cool, man. Tori's just pulling up now."

7

I watched as two chicks got out of a blue beetle and walked over to us. One with dark hair, the other blond. As they strutted our way, I hoped the dark-haired chick was Tori. Because the blond…she was a knockout. I was going to lose my only friend here, if I was crushing on his girl.

"Hey, baby." The dark-haired girl leaned in and gave Chris a quick kiss. I let out a breath of relief, I didn't realize I was holding, and sent up a silent *thank you*.

"Tori, meet Tyler. He's our new quarterback. Tyler meet my girl, Tori." Chris introduced us. "And let's not forget her bestie, Kyla."

"Hey Tori. Kyla." I acknowledged them with a slight lift of my chin, sticking my hands in my pockets. I was gonna play this cool. I hoped Kyla didn't have a boyfriend, but I didn't want to seem like an overanxious asshole.

The chick was tiny. Maybe five foot. She had a tight little body, with curves in all the right places, which I pretended not to notice. I already wanted to wrap my arms around her and see how she felt under my hands.

"Hey, Tyler. Chris says you're pretty amazing on the field. Welcome to Oak Valley," Tori said.

"Amazing, huh?" I smiled.

"Yeah, 'amazing' is not what I said. Don't let it go to your head, dude. But you are pretty good. It's gonna be a great season! Hey, and Kyla is on the cheerleading team, so you two will probably see a lot of each other. Plus, these two," Chris motioned between Tori and Kyla, "are thick as thieves, so if you're gonna hang with me you'll be hanging with the two of them."

I could do that! Endure the hardship. For a friend that is.

"Hey, Tori could do worse for a best friend." Kyla smiled. And what a gorgeous smile it was. "I try to keep her on the straight and narrow. It's a full-time job, especially since she's hooked up with you." Kyla winked and pointed her accusing finger at Chris.

8

"Always the party pooper, Kyla," Chris chided.

"Don't listen to him, Tyler. He knows I've saved their butts more than once. I'm their cover story for all their illicit activities." Kyla laughed.

"Well, nice to meet you, Ky. I guess we'll be hanging together, since this asshole is my only friend so far." I motioned to Chris.

"Damn right. I'm the only one who can put up with your cocky ass," Chris joked.

"Oh, you wound me." I feigned hurt as I clutched my chest. "Right here, man. That hurts." I pounded my fist to my heart. "Don't let this guy give you the wrong impression," I said turning to Kyla. "I'm one of the good guys," I flirted.

"We'll see," she flirted back with a coy smile.

I stood at my locker, looking at my schedule for about the tenth time. World Lit then lunch. Thank God! I stood there trying to remember if I needed to go right or left to find room 408. I looked up and Kyla was at her locker, a few down from mine, grabbing the things for her next class. I contemplated asking her for help. It would be better than walking in circles and for sure being late to my next class.

I approached her as she closed her locker. She jumped back in surprise, when she saw me standing there. Her hand flew up to her chest. "Jesus, you scared the crap out of me," she gasped. "How's your first day going?"

"Alright, I guess." I shrugged. "Hey, can you point me in the right for direction for room 408? I've got World Lit next, with Harrison."

"Really?" she said kind of excited. "Me too!" She linked her arm with mine and dragged me through the hallway. She smelled like the beach... coconut and vanilla. It was intoxicating. I let the smell fill my senses as she led me to class.

She yammered on about something, but I didn't know what. I forced myself to focus. "Harrison's kind of tough. I had him for American Lit in tenth grade. Just make sure you keep up on the reading. He likes to put you on the spot."

"Good to know," I replied as we turned the corner and she led me into the class. There were lots of seats open. Kyla walked right to the front and took a seat in the front row. *Fucking fantastic.* I internally cringed. I looked around the room, seeing an empty seat in the back. I eyed it, but then moved to the seat next to her. If I wanted to get to know her, sitting in the back was not an option.

I watched her as she unpacked her backpack. Her long, blond hair shielded her face from me, as she pulled out her notebook and pens. Yes, pens. As in multiple. A variety of colors. I let out a low laugh.

She turned to look at me. "What's so funny?" she asked, squinting her eyes at me.

I pointed at her array of pens. "Basic black doesn't do it for you, huh?"

"I like to color code, okay? Take it or leave it. It works for me."

I would definitely take it. She was damn cute. "Don't get defensive. I'm not judging. It was just an observation." I reached down to grab my own pen from my backpack. I looked in the front pocket, then the side pocket. Shit! I must have left it in my last class.

I turned back to Kyla, pointing at her pens again. "Do you think I can borrow one of those? I must have left mine in chemistry."

She scooped them up in one hand and fanned them out for me. "Sure. Pick a color." She smiled.

"Thanks." I pretended to contemplate my decision. "I think I'll go with blue." I winked, stealing the pen out of her hand.

# Chapter 3
## Kyla

Cue the butterflies. They were there, making my stomach queasy as we walked to World Lit together day after day. Tyler's dark hair and blue eyes were hypnotizing. His body was strong and muscular. He was tall and made me feel small, but not vulnerable. We had developed an easy friendship. But I just had a feeling. I couldn't shake the thought that something more was to come. Maybe it was just wishful thinking.

He became popular instantly. Tyler was the school hero, pushing our football team's winning record higher than it had ever been. We we're definitely headed for a championship.

Why would he want a mousy, smart girl, when he could clearly have his pick of any girl in the school? God knew I'd seen them shamelessly flirting with him. It was ridiculous, actually, the way those girls threw themselves at him.

Yeah, I was captain of the cheer squad, but guys seemed to know that I wouldn't put out and so I guessed, I wasn't worth the time. Whatever! I wasn't going to compromise myself for a guy that would use me and throw me away.

But I might... for Tyler. Take the chance, that is. He made me feel things I had never felt before. Would it be so awful to be bad with him? No. But would I be able to handle the rejection afterwards? Again... no.

We fell into a routine. Every morning, we met before school. Third hour we had World Lit together and then went to lunch. After school, we both had practice out by the football field. It was hard to concentrate on the cheer routines at practice, when I knew he was just across the field doing his thing. The butterflies became the comforting normal as time went by. Easy laughter and conversation filled our days. I wanted more from him but was too scared to initiate anything. Maybe I was reading too much into his words or the way he placed his hand on the small of my back as we walked to class together. I didn't want to get friend-zoned by our star QB. I could only hope that he had the same feelings for me that I was having for him, and that he would make the first move.

It was October and Homecoming was fast approaching.

At the end of the day, Tyler met up with me at my locker. He looked at me sheepishly. "Kyla, I was wondering if you might want to meet up after practice today? I mean..." he stumbled, "I know it's kind of last minute so if you're busy... I just thought maybe we could grab something to eat."

"No... I mean yes." *Breathe,* I told myself. Taking a deep breath, I started over. "No, I'm not busy and yes, I'll go out to eat with you. Just let me text my mom and dad to let them know."

Relief washed over his face. Seriously? He was nervous? "Meet you by the locker rooms at 4:30?"

"Sounds good," I tried to sound casual.

"Okay, I'll see you then." He turned and jogged down the hallway to practice.

I leaned back against my locker. What was wrong with me? This is what I wanted, and I immediately turned into a bumbling idiot? I needed to pull it together! Maybe it was something, but maybe it was nothing. It was just food, but maybe it was kind of like a date. Maybe?

We arrived at the restaurant and were seated at a booth toward the back. The waitress came over and took our orders. I couldn't help the nervous feeling that was in the pit of my stomach.

"So, I know you're like really smart, and pretty, and a cheerleader," he started, leaning over the table toward me, "but no boyfriend? What's the story with that?"

I nearly choked on my water. "Wow! Nothing like getting right to the point."

"Well, I've known you for what, like a month? I'm just trying to figure you out. It doesn't make sense to me."

I took another long sip from my water, trying to think of how to respond. "I've had boyfriends," I assured him. "I don't know. I spend a lot of time studying. Grades are really important to me. I want to get a scholarship for college, take the pressure off my parents. I just don't have time for something that isn't real. You know?"

"I kind of get that," Tyler answered. "I'm pretty much guaranteed a scholarship for football, but I have to keep my grades up too. I don't want to be the cliché dumb jock."

I relaxed a little bit and leaned across the table on my elbows. "I'm pretty sure you're not. I've seen your grades in World Lit. They're *almost* as good as mine," I said with a smirk.

"Well, maybe if I color coded my notes, I'd do better."

I narrowed my eyes at him. "Are you making fun of me, Tyler Jackson?"

"Never!" He looked offended. "Okay, maybe a little bit," he said flashing me his million-dollar smile.

Just then, the waitress brought our burgers. I was just about to take my first bite, when it happened.

"I was thinking," he said nervously, not really making eye contact. "You wanna go to Homecoming with me? We could double with Tori and Chris. It could be fun."

I had been waiting for Tyler to initiate something. Finally, the invite I had been waiting for. I hoped it was more than just a double date, but I would take what I could get. The butterflies were going crazy, churning in my stomach, ready to take flight. Maybe this made me pathetic, but I didn't care.

I tried to play it cool. "Yeah. Sounds like fun."

"Cool! So, it's a date," he said with a smile.

"It's a date," I confirmed while trying to hide the smile that was dying to break free.

The next couple of weeks flew by. With Tyler being our quarterback and me being captain of the cheer squad I knew all eyes would be on us at the dance. I found the perfect dress. It was a purple halter style, covered in sequins. It hugged my curves and flared out at the bottom. My high heels would make me a little taller, although I would still be dwarfed by Tyler's height and muscular body. I was dying to get my hands on his body. I had never felt so attracted to anyone. It wasn't exactly a mystery what was under those henleys he was constantly wearing. I saw him at practice and running on the track in all his shirtless glory. The toned muscles in his arms and chest went down to a perfect "V" at his hips. High school guys should not have been allowed to look like that. But he did. I wanted nothing more than to run my hands over those muscles.

I liked him. A lot. I just hoped he liked me in the same way. For the first time in my life, I was willing to let go of the "good girl" image I had created for myself. Straight A Student. Rule Follower. Dependable. Virgin. Those were all words that could be used to describe me. I was the girl who was everyone's friend. And I had always been okay with that.

Until now.

I wanted to push boundaries and cross proverbial lines with him. Did he want me the same way, or was I just convenient? That thought rattled around in my brain, even though I knew he could have asked any of the girls that flirted with him on a daily basis. I tried not to think about it. I just wanted to have an awesome night, and so I put it out of my head.

The day of the Homecoming game arrived. I cheered louder than ever before. I knew Tyler could win this game for us. At half time, convertibles lined the track waiting for the Homecoming Court. Both Tyler and I were on Court, but we weren't coupled together. We got in our respective cars, dressed in our uniforms, and made our way around the track. I did my obligatory waves to the crowd as everyone cheered from the stands.

Once we had circled the track, we all exited our cars and stood by the podium on the field—guys on one side, girls on the other. Tyler was almost guaranteed to be crowned king. Even though he was the new kid on the block, football paved the way for his popularity. I was hopeful for myself, but guaranteed? Definitely not.

Finally, the announcer started introducing everyone on the Court. "And the moment everyone has been waiting for. Our Homecoming King and Queen are.... Tyler Jackson and Kyla O'Malley. Congratulations!"

The crowd went crazy. They clapped wildly while hooting and hollering. We made our way to the podium. Tyler was given a ridiculous crown, which he still managed to make look good. A silver jeweled tiara was set on my head and a dozen roses placed in my arms. Tyler put his arm around my waist and kissed my cheek. He leaned towards my ear and whispered, "Can't wait for tonight, baby." I plastered on a smile but couldn't stop the red from creeping up my neck and into my cheeks, even though I knew no one had heard him.

My mind worked overtime, as we posed for pictures and were congratulated. Soon it was time for Tyler to jog back to the locker room. I returned to my squad to finish the rest of the game. All I could think about was him whispering in my ear. *Can't wait for tonight, baby.*

"You look hot!" Tori exclaimed as we got ready for the Homecoming dance. "Tyler is going to totally fall for you tonight."

"You think so," I said timidly. I wasn't used to looking so glamorous, but Tori had pulled out all her magic tricks that night. She curled my long, blond hair in soft, beachy waves and my make-up looked sultry and sexy. I had to admit, I barely recognized the girl in the mirror, but she was hot. I was so ready for this date.

Chris and Tyler showed up at the same time, ready to whisk us off to a night of dancing and who knew what else. My parents took all the requisite photos, bragging about what a *cute couple* we were. When I'd had enough, I made the excuse that we would be late and quickly got us out of there. I was ready for this night to start.

"You look beautiful," Tyler complimented me, as he opened the car door. He was driving a new black Challenger. It was all sleek and muscle, just like him. I swooned just a little before I regained my composure.

"Thank you." I glowed. Tori and Chris would meet us there. I was thankful that we had two separate cars, because I wasn't sure how this night would end. Although I hoped for more, I wasn't sure just how much more. I just wanted more than the platonic relationship we had. But what did *more* mean? I wasn't ready to give up my V card yet. I wasn't sure what he would expect from me. I hoped to find out by the end of the night. And I hoped that he wouldn't be turned off by me not giving it up to him.

# Chapter 4
## Tyler

Wow! Just wow! I was a lucky son of a bitch. This girl was gorgeous, and she was with me. We entered the dance, and I swear heads turned to look at us. We did look pretty good, if I did say so myself. She was the captain of the cheer squad and looked fucking hot. And I, well I was the high school's ticket to a championship season. We looked like the power couple of Oak Valley High. And I guess we were.

I ignored the stares of other guys toward my girl. That's right....my girl. She was mine, at least for the night. She had no idea how beautiful she was, and that made me like her even more. Like? Was that all this was? I wasn't sure. But *more* was definitely a possibility.

We danced all night. Most guys just liked to stand around and shoot the shit while their girls did all the dancing. But I wasn't going to waste this chance with Kyla. She was a great dancer. I loved putting my hands on her hips. I pulled her closer and rocked up against her. When the song slowed to "Trying Not to Love You" by Nickelback, she threw her arms around my neck and my hands went immediately to her waist. I closed my eyes, this song couldn't be any more perfect for the way I was feeling. I pulled her in a little tighter, pressing myself into her, hoping she could feel how she was affecting me. God, this song, coupled with her body, was killing me.

Kyla bit her bottom lip and stared up at me from under her long, dark lashes. "I'm having an awesome time," she whispered. "Thank you for bringing me."

I stared into her green eyes. They were captivating. I was starting to fall for her and I wasn't sure if I could stop it. Damn. I didn't want to stop it.

18

"My pleasure. Trust me." I shifted my hands lower, so they were resting on her ass. I'd been waiting to feel it under my hands and I had to give it a little squeeze. Her tight little body stiffened, then relaxed at my touch. I was going to have to go slow. My instincts told me she was as innocent as she looked. Getting antsy, I lower my mouth to her ear. "You about ready to get out of here? I want to spend some alone time with you before I take you home."

Her breath hitched, but she slowly nodded yes. I wrapped her hand in mine and started toward the door.

"Whoa! Where do you two think you're going? Cutting out early on us is not cool," Tori teased. We'd been caught! So much for sneaking outta here.

"Tyler and I are just… well the dance is almost over anyway. Talk to you in the morning?" Kyla asked over her shoulder.

"Definitely. And I'll want details, girl!" Tori yelled. I led Kyla toward the door. I turned around just in time to see Chris give a raised eyebrow and a chin lift. Was that a vote of confidence or a warning? I wasn't sure. I needed to go slow with Kyla. She was trusting and vulnerable…God, I hoped I wouldn't fuck this up.

I got her situated in the car then rounded to open the driver's side, letting out a puff of anxiety. I gave myself a little pep talk. *Take it slow. Don't scare her off. She's worth the wait.*

I got in and started the car, focusing on the smooth rumble of its engine. "Where to, beautiful?"

"Umm… there's a park a couple of blocks from my house. How about there?"

"Sounds good!"

# Chapter 5
## Kyla

*What the hell am I doing?* I was so out of my league here. God, why didn't I talk to Tori about this? She'd know what to do. Yeah, right! She'd tell me to go for it. She'd been busting my ass about that damn V card for months. I was so not her and I was so not ready! I wished I had that confidence.

Okay, this was getting awkward. We'd been parked for...how long? And I still hadn't said a word. Instead, I sat there like a scared rabbit. I turned to look at him. He was already looking at me. His dark hair was spiked up in front, making me want to run my hands through it. I stared into those blue eyes and got kind of lost.

"I'm not gonna bite, Kyla."

"I know, obviously. It's just...I don't normally do this," I stuttered.

"Do what? We haven't even done anything yet." Then he flashed that smile. One side of his mouth rose up and showed off that damn adorable dimple.

I threw my hands up in exasperation. "This! All of this! Parking in a dark lot! Sitting next to a hot guy in a car late at night!"

"You think I'm hot?" Tyler laughed, full on smiling now.

"Seriously? That's what you got out of what I just said?" I sighed. "And yes, I think you're hot."

"Well, at least you're talking now." He unbuckled his seatbelt and scooted closer to me, leaning over the console. He moved in further, coming in for a kiss. A kiss I desperately wanted. He ran his hand up my arm to my shoulder, then gently cupped my face. He pressed his lips against mine and let his

20

tongue explore my mouth. I returned the kiss and let my tongue mingle with his. I got lost in it. It became feverish and frantic. I let out an involuntary moan, as I felt my lady parts clench. His kiss sent an electric shock through me, right to my core.

I put my hand on his chest and gently pushed him back. "Look, Tyler, I like you. A lot! And I don't want this to make things weird between the two of us. So, if you don't feel the same way, tell me now. I don't want to screw with our friendship. Because we're starting to cross a line here."

He looked in my eyes. "I like you too, Kyla. And I want more than a friendship. I want you to be my girl."

His girl? Yesss! "I wanna be your girl, but I don't know what I'm doing here." I was totally messing this up. "It's just that.... well...I've never...you know..." I stumbled over my words. "I'm a virgin!" I blurted. I dropped my head into my hands and felt the color creep up my neck into my cheeks. Could I be anymore mortified? If I could have crawled under the seat, I would have. Kill. Me. Now!

I felt his finger come up under my chin to lift my head. I peered at him from under my lashes. My embarrassment was evident. "It's okay, baby. Me too," he said softly.

"You too, what?" I asked.

"I'm a virgin too," he whispered.

"Really?"

"Really. We take this as slow as you need. I'm not gonna lie. I want you, but you call the shots," he said, searching my eyes for understanding.

"Okay."

He leaned toward me, holding my face in his hands. "I'm gonna kiss you again now. That okay?"

"Yes." My voice was raspy and breathless. "More than okay."

His lips met mine gently. Softly. His tongue traced along my bottom lip and slipped inside my mouth. Our tongues searched and twisted together in a gentle dance. I pressed further, deepening the kiss as his hands ran through my hair. He gently tugged, and another moan escaped me. I felt my panties getting wet. What was this boy doing to me? I was pretty sure little red hearts were floating around my head. The kiss seemed to go on forever. His lips traveled down the side of my mouth, over my chin. I leaned my head back to give him better access as he kissed my neck.

Reluctantly he pulled back. "I better take you home, or I won't be the good guy I just promised you," he admitted.

"You are a good guy. Thank you for making this night perfect." I'm sure the smile plastered on my face was ridiculous, but there was no controlling it.

He drove the few short blocks to my house and parked. He came around to open my door and took my hand to lead me up the front walk. When we got to the door I turned to him and he took my face in his hands. He gave me a gentle last kiss. "Best first date ever."

"Good night, Tyler," I said, bringing my fingers up to touch my swollen lips.

"Good night, sweet Kyla." He turned and walked back to his car.

I quietly turned the knob, opened the door, and crept up to my bedroom. I spun in a circle and flopped back on my bed. I was in love!

# Chapter 6
## Tyler

"So, you and Kyla, huh?" Chris said, as he spotted me while I was bench pressing. I let out an exasperated breath as I pushed the weight up and back to set it on the stand.

"Yeah. What about it?" I taunted.

"Nothing, man. Just asking. Defensive a little?" He smirked. "Where'd you two disappear to last night anyway?"

I moved to the leg-lift machine and adjusted the weight. I sat down and started lifting, pushing myself just a little harder. "Just stopped at this park by her house. Talked. You know?"

"Talked, huh? That what you're calling it? She and Tori have been on the phone all morning. I know something's going on."

"What? You want me to share with you, like we're a couple of chicks? Feeling left out?" I had 20 more reps to go. I pushed harder.

"Nah, man. It's just that Kyla's a sweet girl. I don't want to see her getting hurt. Plus, if this goes bad, Tori will tear my balls off for introducing you two. And I kind of like my balls right where they are."

I dropped the weight down. "What? In her hands?" I joked.

"Better in her hands than my own, if you know what I mean?" he shot back, grinning like a Cheshire cat.

"Yeah, I got it." I gave him a pointed look. "It's not like that with her. I like her, dude. A lot. We agreed to take it slow. I'm not gonna touch her unless she's ready. But the waiting…it's probably gonna kill me."

"Death by blue balls, huh?"

23

"Very funny, fucker! But seriously, I'm not gonna hurt her. Your balls are safe for now," I assured him as I moved on to the free weights.

"Good to know." Chris moved over to the leg-lift machine I had just abandoned. "Hey, you hear back from that scout from Michigan State?"

"Yeah…they're offering me a full ride to play football at MSU next year. I think I'm gonna take it." How could I pass up that opportunity? It's what I had been working for since I was a kid. I grew up watching football on TV with my dad, hoping one day it would be me. This could be my ticket to the pros, if I played my cards right.

"How's that going to look if this thing with you and Kyla works?" Chris questioned.

"First of all, I haven't even made it to second base with her yet." I glared at him. Not that I needed to explain myself to him. "Secondly, if this does work out, and I hope it does, she's been talking about going to Western Michigan. WMU is only an hour and a half drive. I think we can make that work."

"Yeah. I guess you're right. Tori and I are looking at WMU too. It's not that far. We'll still be able to hang, right? …even if you are the big man on campus."

"I'll be a little fish in a big pond, brother. Freshman. Even with the scholarship, I'll probably be sitting the bench most of the first year. I think I'll have time." We knuckle bumped, as an understanding passed between us. Going to different schools wouldn't keep us from being friends.

I didn't know what the future would bring. I just knew I wanted Kyla to be part of it.

# Chapter 7
## Kyla

The next few weeks were a whirlwind. Tyler and I spent more and more time together. Kissing him was like nothing I had ever experienced before. There was so much feeling and passion behind our kisses that at times I felt like I would explode. My heart would beat faster and the urges inside of me started to become unbearable. I decided I wanted to go a little further with Tyler. I wasn't ready for sex, but I wanted to explore my sexuality with him.

Tyler took Oak Valley High to the Michigan High School State Championship, just as he had promised he would. We were playing Cass Tech High School in the championship game. The game was held in downtown Detroit, at Ford Field. Both the cheerleaders and the football players loaded onto a bus for the game, and the energy was electric. I sat next to Ty on the bus and snuggled into his side. No matter how many people were around, we always seemed to be in our own little world.

"You nervous?" I asked.

"Yes and no," he answered honestly. "Yes, because it is the State Championship game. No, because the team has done so well this year. I really think we can do this. Cass Tech is tough, but so are we." Tyler kissed the top of my head and squeezed me a little tighter.

"You know I'll be cheering for you tonight. After all, you are my favorite player. I mean the competition was tough," I teased, "but I like you best."

Tyler grabbed me around the waist and set me on his lap. "Is that so? And what is it that you like so much about me?" He teased back.

"Well…" I pretended to think about it. "For one, you look damn cute in your uniform. You have a nice ass." I looked down at him and bit my lip.

Tyler reached up and pulled my lip from under my teeth. I knew it drove him crazy when I bit my lip. "So that's it? You like me for my body?"

I shook my head. "That's not all. You make me laugh and smile. You make me happy when I'm with you. And…you're an incredible kisser."

"Oh, yeah?"

I nodded. "Yeah," I whispered.

Tyler pulled my head down and kissed me deeply, pushing his tongue inside my mouth. God, I loved his kisses.

"Get a room, you two!" Chris leaned over the seat and interrupted our kiss.

Tyler gave him a stern look. "If you don't like it, don't look!"

"Hey, I just don't want her to give you a hard-on. I don't want you breaking your pecker during the game." Chris laughed.

Ty put his hand on Chris's head and pushed him back down into his seat. "Very funny, fucker!"

I couldn't help the giggle that escaped me. "Could that really happen?" I asked innocently.

"I suppose so. I really don't want to find out." He gave me a quick peck and set me on the seat beside him. "So, what do you want to do after the game tonight?"

"You're not hanging out with the guys after the game?"

"I could, but I'd rather spend time with my girl. Are you okay with that?"

I loved when he called me his girl. It made my heart flutter in my chest. "I'd like that. I'd like to spend some time alone with you." I leaned close to his ear. "I'd like to do a little more than kissing."

Tyler pulled his head back and quirked his eyebrow at me. "Are you serious?"

26

I nodded again and leaned back close to his ear. "I'm not ready to go all the way, but I'm ready for a little more."

Tyler smiled at me and adjusted himself. "You're not really helping the situation in my pants."

When we got to Ford Field, the players headed to the locker room and the cheerleaders towards the field. I gave Ty a quick, chaste kiss for luck and we went our separate ways. I really did love him. I hadn't said the words yet and neither had he. But I was sure we both felt the same way.

We had about an hour to wait before the game started. All the girls on the squad were hyped about tonight's game. The sheer size of Ford Field was amazing. I led the squad through our stretches and then we practiced some of our newest cheers. I was really going to miss cheerleading. Tonight, was my last night as the captain of our squad and I'd have been lying if I said I wasn't a little sad about it.

Maybe next year I could cheer at Western. I was torn about it. On one hand I would be able to continue doing something I really loved and was good at. But on the other hand, if Tyler and I were still dating, I would miss all his games at Michigan State. I would have to see where our relationship was at when it was time for tryouts.

It was time for the game to start. The stadium was pretty full for a high school game. The cheerleaders formed a tunnel for the guys to run through on their way to the field. They announced the starters by name and the crowd cheered loudly for each of the players. We had won the coin toss and our team chose to receive first. We took an early lead in the game, while Cass Tech tried to play catch up through the first half.

When the second half started, Cass Tech came out strong. They quickly tied up the score and then took the lead. When we finally tied the score, there were only a few minutes left in the game. There was a good chance the game would go into overtime. Cass Tech took possession. Their quarterback threw a nice pass and their wide receiver caught it, then fumbled! Chris picked up the ball and ran toward our end zone. Our guys covered him expertly, clearing a path. Everyone was holding their breath as Chris flew down the field. With just seconds left on the clock, he crossed into the end zone and threw the ball down on the field! The team ran and jumped on him, practically knocking Chris over with their enthusiasm. We had just won the State Championship!

# Chapter 8
## Tyler

Oh my, God! What a rush! I didn't think we were going to pull it off, but the last few minutes of the game were incredible. When their receiver fumbled the ball and Chris picked it up, I swear everyone was on their feet screaming. I was so excited for Chris. I knew that play would be highlighted on television for days. Every channel would be replaying it. Chris deserved all the attention he was going to get for the touchdown. That was the way to go out as a senior!

After we showered, we met the girls back on the bus. Kyla hadn't put her sweats back on, so she was only wearing her tiny cheer skirt over her legs when I scooted into the seat next to her.

I loved her legs. They were short little things, but they were toned and beautiful. Since we'd started dating, Kyla and I often went running together. It was another excuse for us to spend time with each other. We'd usually run to some secluded area, make out, and then head back. She was gorgeous when her face was free of makeup and natural. And her running outfits gave me a better glimpse of what she was hiding underneath her clothes. I was falling more in love with her every day.

I put my hand on her thigh and she threw her arms around my neck. "Congratulations, baby!"

I wrapped my arms around her and pulled her in tight. I loved feeling her pressed up against me. "Thanks, Ky! I didn't know if we were going to pull it off. Did you see that run Chris made? It must have been about seventy yards."

"Of course, I saw it! Everyone was holding their breath until he made it into the end zone. It really was amazing!"

29

Chris popped his head over the seat behind us. He had a shit-eating grin on his face. "I heard the word amazing. You must be talking about me!" He waggled his eyebrows up and down.

"I was," Kyla said. "That was really great! I'm so happy for you." She turned and gave him a quick peck on the cheek.

"You guys are coming out to celebrate with us, right? We're all going to IHOP. Tori's going to meet us there."

I looked at Kyla questioningly. I knew I had said I didn't want to hang with the guys and I would spend time with her, but we had just won the biggest game of the season. She didn't even hesitate. "Of course, were coming! We wouldn't miss it!"

"Cool! I'll let Tori know you'll be there." Chris sank back into his seat and began texting.

I really was in love with Kyla. She could have easily said we had other plans. She never made me have to choose between football and her. "Thanks, babe. I know I promised you some one-on-one time."

She waved me off. "I'm gonna text my parents and see if they'll extend my curfew. I don't want you to miss the celebration. We can spend time together after that." She pulled out her phone and started texting.

"You sure?"

"Of course! It's not like you win the State Championship every day."

I leaned over and gave her a sweet kiss. "You really are perfect. You know that?"

She just smiled back at me when she was finished on her phone. "Done. I don't have to be home until two. That will give us plenty of time."

I put my arm around her waist and pulled her close. She rested her head on my chest, while I had my hand on her thigh up under her skirt. I loved holding her like this.

We met everyone at IHOP and stayed for about an hour. Even though I wanted to celebrate with the guys, I wanted to be

30

alone with my girl even more. "You want to go to the park?" I asked her. That was our usual place. It was dark and secluded. No one ever bothered us there. We'd spent a lot of time making out in the backseat of my car at that park.

"Yeah."

I couldn't get what she had told me out of my mind. I wanted to do a lot more with Kyla, but I'd settle for whatever she was willing to give. I always let her set the boundaries. It wasn't easy. I felt like I was walking around with a permanent hard-on. I was an almost eighteen-year-old guy and sex was always on my mind, especially with someone like Ky. She was smart, sexy, and fun. I felt like we had a special bond that connected us together. She wasn't like any other girl I had ever dated.

I pulled into the park and drove around to the back where I knew no one would bother us. I turned the radio on low, so we could still talk, but honestly talking was the last thing I wanted to do. Kyla crawled over the console into the back seat. Her ass stuck up in the air, showing off the briefs under her skirt. I gave her ass a playful swat. "I would have opened the door for you. You didn't have to crawl over the console." I followed her lead and crawled into the back too, which was a little more difficult for me, considering I was six-foot two and she was barely five-foot tall.

I loosened the tie, coach had insisted we wear, and threw it back in the front seat. Kyla unbuttoned the top few buttons on my dress shirt. It was sexy when she undressed me like that. "I'm so proud of you," she said. "Are you going to accept the scholarship from Michigan State?"

"I have to let them know by January. But yeah, I think I am. Are you still thinking about Western?"

"They have a really great graphic design program. I mean, I could really do anything, but I love the creativity and I'm good at it. I want to do something I love for the rest of my life. I don't want to be stuck in some stuffy office."

"I know what you mean. I'm going to major in business management, but I'd really love to play pro-ball. The degree is a backup plan. Can you imagine getting paid to play football? That would be a dream come true."

"You'll do it," she said confidently. "You have the drive and the talent. One day I'll be watching you on television and I'll be able to say I knew you way back when you were just a nobody."

"A nobody? Thanks a lot!" I laughed.

"You know what I mean." She swatted me on the chest, and I grabbed her wrists. I placed her arms around my waist, and I leaned in to kiss her. I held the back of her head and pulled her into me. Her hand slipped inside my shirt and rubbed my chest. The kiss became heated quickly as I devoured her lips and tongue. Kyla leaned back on the seat and I followed her. I was practically laying on top of her in the cramped back seat of my car.

"Ty?"

"Yes," I said breathlessly.

"I want you to touch me. I need more," she begged.

"What do you want from me?" I asked. I stared into her green eyes and searched for what she wanted.

Kyla took my hand and placed it up under the top of her uniform, on her stomach. "I want you to touch me here," she answered. She moved my hand higher, until it was right below her tits. "Please...touch me."

I reached my hand up higher and took her tits in my hand. I rubbed her on top of her sports bra. They were so soft and full. I couldn't see her, but I could feel her, and that was enough. She wasn't super big, but they were big for her small size. Just a handful and it was all I needed. I had fantasized about touching her boobs for so long. I could feel her nipples harden under her bra and I ran my fingers over them.

"Go under my bra. Please," she gasped.

32

I moved my hand down and found the edge of her sports bra. It fit her tightly, but I managed to slip my hand underneath. I palmed her tit and rolled her nipple between my fingers. She felt like heaven in my hand. I worked one, then moved to the other. Kyla threw her head back and let out a soft moan. It was the sexiest sound I ever heard. "Oh my, God. That feels so good."

"Baby, you're killing me here. Your tits feel amazing. I've wanted to touch you for so long." I took her hand and put it on the front of my pants, so she could feel my erection. "See what you do to me?"

Kyla became bold, and she undid the top button of my pants. "I want to feel you," she said. She pulled the zipper down and placed her hand inside my pants, over my boxer briefs. She rubbed me up and down. I was thick and long, and I let her feel every inch of me. Her fingers played with the waist band and she looked at me to ask permission. I nodded, and her hand slipped inside. Her small fingers grasped me and stroked me up and down. The feeling was unbelievable. Her fingertips rubbed over the precum that beaded on the tip of my dick and she rubbed it down along my shaft. After a few minutes, I couldn't take any more. "Baby, you gotta stop or I'm going to come all over your hand." I pulled her hand from my pants and kissed her palm.

"I want to make you feel good," she cooed.

"You do, but let's save that for another night." I couldn't believe I was the one putting the brakes on, but I didn't want to push the limits with her. Her pleasure was my first priority. "Let me make you feel good."

"You already have," she said innocently.

"Ky, I want to touch you here." I reached under her skirt and ran my fingers along the edge of her briefs at the inside of her hip. These things were like glorified underwear that covered her most intimate areas. I moved to the floorboards in the back of the car and kneeled. I laid Kyla on the backseat with her knees slightly bent. I whispered in her ear, "Has anybody ever made you come before?" She shook her head with big innocent eyes.

"Have you ever made yourself come?" She shook her head again and buried her face into the back of the seat. "We don't have to do this," I told her. Even though I was still a virgin, I'd done this before. I knew how to make her feel good.

"Kiss me," she said. "I want you to touch me, but I need you to distract me. I can't think about it."

I leaned forward and kissed her deeply. She grabbed the back of my head and pulled me in tighter. We got lost in the kiss and then I moved my hand up under her skirt again. I moved my hand along the edge of her briefs and pushed inside. I felt her soft folds under my fingers and moved down further until my hand was between her legs. She was soaking wet. I rubbed over her wetness and then slowly slipped a finger inside her. Her breath hitched, and she tightened around my finger. "Relax, baby." She did, and I inserted another finger into her. I pumped my fingers in and out of her slowly.

Kyla arched up off the seat. "Oh, my...more." I slid my fingers out of her and slid them up to her folds. I found the soft nub hidden in there and rubbed her wetness over it. She writhed beneath my hand. All of a sudden, she tensed up. "Stop...I can't take any more." I immediately pulled my hand out of her briefs. "I'm sorry," she said. She sat up and wrapped her arms around my shoulders, burying her head in my neck.

I rubbed her back gently. "Don't be sorry. If you're not ready for this, you're not ready. I'm not going to get upset with you. I only want to make you happy."

"You do. It's just...I thought I was ready, but I'm not."

I got up from the floorboards and sat on the seat next to her. I pulled her onto my lap and looked into her eyes, so she would know I meant what I said. "Kyla, I love you. I'll wait for as long as it takes for you be ready. I don't want to rush you."

Her eyes softened. "You love me?"

I nodded. "Yeah, I do. I love everything about you."

"I love you, too. I'm not trying to be a tease. I just… need more time."

"There's no rush, Ky."

# Chapter 9
## Kyla

Fall turned to winter and winter turned to spring. Our senior year was flying by and Tyler and I fell madly in love. Yes, we were undeniably in love. I had wanted the butterflies in my stomach, the stars in my eyes, the head over heels kind of love. And I'd found that with Tyler. We were practically inseparable. When you saw one of us, the other wasn't far behind.

I laid on my bed, drawing in my sketchbook, thinking about us. I drew a flaming heart, with butterflies spreading their colorful wings flying from the center. I spent extra time shading it in with reds, yellows, blues, and purples. I looked at my drawing, thinking it captured my feelings about Tyler.

Our relationship had moved way past kissing. God, I loved kissing Tyler. Feeling his strong lips on mine and his gentle touch. I felt safe in his strong arms, like nothing could hurt me. I let him feel me up. I had let him move his hands up under my blouse, and under my bra. I loved his hands rubbing against my breasts. Wanting. Kneading. They gently brushed over my nipples and made me moan. When he put his hand between my legs, he rubbed in places that got me so wet. His fingers inside me felt so good. It took some time, but I finally let him make me come. I didn't know it would be so amazing! And I let him do it again and again.

I'd made him come, too. I'd been rubbing his dick in the back of his car and his hand was down my pants. We'd gotten so carried away, that neither one of us was thinking. I knew he wanted it as bad as I did. Without warning, I felt him come all over my hand. He felt bad about it, but I didn't. I wanted to make him feel as good as he made me feel.

Despite all our touching, our clothes had never come off. We never breached that boundary. I knew he wanted to go all the way, but he never pushed me. He let me set the pace, true to his promise. I could tell that he was getting frustrated. Hell, I was getting frustrated. I wanted his hands all over my naked body. I wanted to see all of him and for him to see all of me. I wanted to know what it would feel like for him to be buried deep inside me.

I loved him.

I looked around my room at all the things that had made up my childhood. The pink curtains and bedspread. The butterflies hanging on the walls. They were symbols of a young girl. I was turning into a woman. I was ready to let the butterflies that hung so quietly… waiting…to fly free and spread their wings. I had held on to my virginity tightly. I was afraid letting go would make me feel dirty. Slutty. I was ready to let go of those thoughts…because Ty made me feel loved, not cheap or slutty. I wanted to share this with him. I was ready!

I shot off a quick text:

*Ky: C U 2nite?*
*Ty: Where else would I be?*
*Ky: Got something important to tell you. Pick me up at 5?*
*Ty: See you then. You OK?*
*Ky: Better than OK. Talk to you tonight.*
*Ty: K. Luv u!*
*Ky: Luv u 2!*

I heard the rumble of the engine right before five. I headed down the stairs, with a bounce in my step and nervous energy running through my body. I stopped in the kitchen where my parents were just sitting down for dinner.

"You heading out with Tyler tonight?" My dad questioned. "I like that boy, but he better not hurt my little girl."

"Oh dad, really? We're just going to get some food, then maybe a movie. We're meeting up with Tori and Chris later."

"Leave her alone," my mom interjected, swatting him on the arm. "Don't you remember what we were like at that age? Young and in love?"

"Yeah." My dad scrunched his eyebrows. "I remember exactly what we were like. That's why I worry." His gaze shifted to me like he was reading my mind, knowing all the thoughts rolling around in there. *Ewww! Get out of my head dad! You don't belong there right now!*

I plastered on a smile and gave my dad a tight hug. "Don't worry. I'm fine."

Just then the doorbell rang. Saved by the bell! I opened the door and Tyler walked through in his usual jeans and henley. My mom walked over and gave Tyler a quick hug. "You two have fun tonight!"

"Thanks Mrs. O'Malley. I'll take good care of Kyla."

"I'm trusting you Tyler. Be safe with my daughter," my dad interjected, a little harsher than necessary.

"Always, Mr. O'Malley. No worries!" Tyler said, looking a little confused.

We made a quick exit and escaped down the walk to Tyler's waiting car. "Okaaay, that was a little weird. What's up with your dad?"

"I think he's realizing that I'm growing up, and he's not too cool with it. My parents were high school sweethearts and I showed up seven months after graduation," I explained.

"Ooooh…that would explain the 'be safe with my daughter' comment." Tyler laughed while imitating my dad. "No worries there, Mr. O'Malley," he mocked. "Where to, beautiful?"

"Mind if we stop at the park before eating? I really want to talk to you about something."

"Oh shit, sorry babe! I totally forgot. Your dad threw me off. I wasn't ready for that. You okay?"

"Yeah, everything's good. More than good, actually."

We drove to the park and walked over to some picnic tables away from listening ears, and sat down on top. I sat cross-legged, while Ty sat the same way across from me. I certainly didn't need an audience for this. I was kind of scared about saying the words out loud. Because then it would be real. I bit at my lip. How was I going to start this awkward conversation? *Just say it*! I told myself.

"What's up? You look nervous. You know you can tell me anything, right? I love you." Tyler questioned. He pulled at my lip, releasing it from my teeth.

"I know, and I love you!" I leaned over and gave him a quick peck on the lips. "And that's why I have to tell you this." I took a deep breath and let it out. "You know how you said my dad had nothing to worry about?" Tyler nodded. "Well, he might. I'm ready!" I looked at him waiting for a reaction. *Please don't make me spell this out.*

Confusion crossed his face and then it lit up in understanding. "Really? Are you saying what I think you're saying? I promised not to push you and I'm going to keep that promise. Are you sure about this?"

"I'm sure!" I nodded eagerly. "One hundred percent sure. I want my first time to be with someone I love. And I love you. I can't imagine being more in love than I am right now."

"Baby, I'm... I don't know what to say. I wasn't expecting this. Hoping, but not expecting."

"Are you happy? I mean, I know this probably wasn't how you were planning... and it's not very... just...," I rambled.

"Ky! Stop talking. I'm happy. More than happy actually." He cradled my face in his hands and looked into my eyes. "But this isn't going to be some quickie in the back of my car. I'm gonna make it special for you. For us. We only get one first time and I want you to remember it with no regrets."

39

"I'm not going to have regrets." I said shaking my head. "As long as I'm with you. That's all that matters. So, when should this special night happen?"

Tyler contemplated our options. "Prom? It's at the Hilton. I'll get us a room."

I pulled back in mocked shock. "Are you asking me to prom, Mr. Jackson?" I gasped in a southern drawl.

"Why, I think I am Miss O'Malley. Is it a date?"

"Yes!" I exclaimed, practically jumping into his arms.

# Chapter 10
## Tyler

"Your brother rocks, man," I said to Chris as I looked at our hotel room. "I can't believe he hooked us up like this." Chris's brother had booked us two rooms and got us champagne and vodka for prom night.

"Yeah, he's cool. He said someone did it for him when he was a senior and he was just passing it on," he replied.

Chris and I stopped at the hotel early to drop some stuff off in our rooms. Candles...check. Champagne and glasses...check. Vodka, just in case the nerves got me...check. Condoms...double check. I was going to make this night special for Ky. Something she would never forget. After waiting this long, nothing was going to mess this up. Except maybe my own nerves. Yeah, I admitted to myself, I was a little scared too. I just wanted everything to live up to her expectations, including me.

"You alright, man? You're looking a little green. Cold feet?" Damn Chris, fucking nothing got by him. He was a little too observant.

"Yeah, I'm good. Just don't want to fuck this up for her."

"Tori and me... our first time was in the back of my dad's pickup. Not exactly romantic, but memorable. I got an elbow in the eye. That girl's a wild cat when it comes to sex." Chris laughed at the memory.

"I feel like a pussy, admitting this...but tonight's gonna be a first for me.

"I kinda figured that out already. Ain't no way a guy who's already had sex, is gonna wait as long as you did for Kyla. I get it though. She's as innocent as they come. Trust me you'll be fine. You're doing this up right," Chris encouraged. "Just do your thing, man. It ain't that hard." He turned serious. "Word of advice?"

"Sure, shoot. I guess it couldn't hurt," I answered honestly.

"Don't go for the gold right off the bat. Girls want to feel special, like they're not being used. Pay attention to the details, make her come first. You make her happy, and she'll sure as shit make you happy." He patted me on the back and started walking to the car. Turning back, he smirked. "Oh, and Tyler…don't forget to wrap your junk!"

I rolled my eyes. That smart ass never passed up an opportunity to bust my balls. But if I was being honest, our "talk" had just made me more jittery.

Chris was right though. It wasn't that hard. The only thing hard was me, thinking about tonight and getting inside Kyla's tight little body. *Make her happy.* Yeah. I could do that.

# Chapter 11
## Kyla

"Your chariot awaits, my lady." Ty ushered me out to his freshly washed and waxed black Challenger, looking sexy in his tuxedo. I was so used to seeing him in jeans and t-shirts that the sight of him in a tux took me back a little. I really was a lucky girl.

Tori and I had spent the day getting mani-pedis and our hair done. Upon her advice, god help me, I had shaved everything. A first for me. Tori and I told our parents we were spending the night at each other's houses. We'd been doing it since third grade, so they didn't even bat an eye. I was ready. I wanted to make sure everything was perfect for tonight.

"Thank you, Mr. Jackson," I smiled at him coyly as he opened my door.

"Your quite welcome, Miss O'Malley."

Tyler ran around to the driver's side and slid in next to me. "Kyla, you look beautiful tonight. Sexy as sin. I can't wait to strip you out of that strapless dress later." He looked at me hungrily.

My heart skipped a beat as my eyes went wide. Those damn butterflies started to take flight in my stomach. Pushing it all back down, I pulled it together. "All in good time, baby. We've got a dance to go to first."

He turned the key in the ignition and the engine rumbled to life. "Hell, yeah! You ready to shake that groove thang, girl?" He wiggled his eyebrows up and down and gave me that million-dollar smile. His dimples were front and center.

"You know I'm ready." I giggled. "How 'bout you, you ready to shake it?"

"Hey, I got moves," he said, focusing back on the road.

I laughed. "Yeah, I know you do." The easy banter back and forth helped to keep the butterflies at bay. I focused on the dance and hanging out with our friends and put the rest out of my mind. For now.

The night was magical. Everything was decorated in blue and silver from the floor to the ceiling. A banner across the front of the ballroom read *A Night to Remember*. It was fitting because I knew I would remember this night forever. We ate. We danced. We laughed. Everything was perfect.

We strolled out onto the dance floor when Lifehouse's "You and Me" came on. We slow danced as Tyler held me tight, pushing his bulging erection into my stomach. I loved that I could do this to him. Suddenly he twirled me around and dipped me low. His face was just inches above mine as I leaned back in his strong arms. He held me steady as he placed a gentle kiss on my lips. "See, I told you I've got moves."

"You trying to impress me?" I asked breathlessly, as he pulled me back up.

"Depends. Is it working?"

I stared up into those deep blue eyes. "Definitely," I whispered.

"You ain't seen nothing yet, baby," he promised, making my insides go all quivery.

After a few more songs, we we're both ready to go. The anticipation was killing me—a mix of excitement and apprehension. I'd seen Chris and Tori sneak out earlier, heading up to their room. "You ready to get out of here, beautiful?" Tyler suggested. I nodded and he led me out of the ballroom, and over to the bank of elevators. Pushing the up button, we waited anxiously for the doors to open. We stepped in and he quickly pulled me in tight, wrapping his strong arms around me. Even in my four-inch heels, I only came up to his chest. "I've been waiting for this all week, baby," he said softly into my ear.

"Me too," I admitted. Just as the doors were about to close, an older couple stepped into the elevator with us. Shit! They looked at us and smiled. I wondered if they knew what we were about to do. I held my breath and stiffened as redness crept up my neck.

Tyler leaned down and whispered in my ear, "Relax, Ky." And I did. I leaned back into his chest, letting his warmth comfort me. The elevator stopped, and the older couple got out on their floor. When the doors closed again, I let out a breath of relief.

"Do you think they knew?" I asked.

"Probably, but it doesn't matter. It's just you and me." The doors opened again, and Tyler wrapped his hand around mine and led me down the hall. He reached in his pocket, pulled out the key card and swiped it, letting us into our room.

I stepped in and froze. There in the center of the room was a king-size bed. My eyes went wide, and I looked away, scanning the rest of the room. I noticed my overnight bag sitting on the desk. I was thankful the guys had brought it up earlier, so I didn't have to worry about it. I stepped in further. The reality was setting in. This would be the last night of my virginity. This was it.

Tyler stepped up behind me. "You okay? If you want to change your mind…"

I spun around to face him. "I don't want to change my mind. I'm ready. I just need a minute." I held my finger up and then pointed to the bathroom.

"Take your time. We've got all night."

I stepped into the bathroom, shutting the door behind me. I looked in the mirror. My eyes were wide, and my cheeks were flushed. *What the hell are you doing?* I asked the girl in the mirror. Holding onto the counter, I hung my head. *You can do this. You can do this. You can do this.* I repeated the silent mantra to myself.

After a few minutes, I raised my head, stood tall and looked back at the girl in the mirror. She was sexy and confident. I quickly wiped under my eyes, patted my cheeks, and pressed my lips together. I was ready to spread my wings and fly.

I opened the door and shut off the light. Stepping out into the room, I gasped in surprise. Soft music played in the background and candles were lit all around the room, casting a soft glow. Tyler stood there in the shadows, holding out a glass of champagne to me.

"Tyler, this is perfect!" I said, bringing my hands up to cover my gasp.

He handed me the glass. "I wanted to make this night special for my girl. Thank you for sharing this with me tonight."

My heart swooned a little more and I felt warmth spreading through my chest and down to my toes. This was what love felt like. And suddenly, all my apprehension disappeared. I took a drink of the champagne and swirled it around my tongue. Then another, for courage. I handed the glass back to Tyler and stepped forward, so we were just inches apart. I looked up at him from under my long lashes, as my hands reached around the back of my dress. I slowly pulled the zipper down, closed my eyes and let the dress fall to my ankles.

# Chapter 12
## Tyler

*HOLY FUCK!*

.

# Chapter 13
## Kyla

Tyler's jaw dropped as he took me in. "You are beautiful, Kyla. I always knew but seeing you like this is just... breathtaking."

I stood there before him in my black strapless bra, lacy black thong, and four-inch heels. I felt sexy and alive for the first time. I stepped out of my dress that was puddled on the floor and took the champagne glasses from his hands. I took a long sip and set them on the dresser.

Tyler seemed frozen in place. I turned to him. "You like?" I took his hands and put them on my sides. I guided them down past my waist and over my hips. I reached up, put my hands on his shoulders up under his tux jacket, and eased it down his arms and dropped it to the floor.

His hands reached for my ass and he lifted me like I was weightless. I wrapped my legs around his waist. He carried me to the bed and set me down gently. He reached up to take off his tie as I started to slip the buttons on his shirt through the holes. Tyler kneeled down on the floor in front of me, making quick work of the rest of his buttons and shrugging out of his shirt.

He reached up and gently rubbed my legs, down from my hips to my ankles and carefully removed one shoe, then the other. He kissed the inside arch of my foot, up my calf, under my knee, and up my thigh to my hip. He eased me onto my back as he continued placing light kisses up my stomach, between my breasts, up my neck and made his way to my lips. His kiss became fiercer, as he devoured my mouth. I opened up to let his tongue twist together with mine. Letting out a moan, I moved my hands to roam across his chest, feeling his muscles under my hands.

Tyler stood, undid his pants, and removed them, all the while keeping his eyes glued to mine. I scooted up the bed 'til my head reached the pillow and unclipped my blond hair, letting it fall gently across my shoulders. I looked at Tyler, as he stood there in only his boxer briefs. His cock strained against the fabric.

He went to his bag, took out a condom and set it on the nightstand. He placed one knee on the bed and crawled up 'til he hovered above me. He stared down at me, my green eyes locked to his blue eyes. All my confidence from before started to drain away and fear crept in. Instead of feeling sexy, I felt exposed. "I'm scared," I whispered.

"I'm not going to hurt you, baby. You tell me to stop, and I'll stop. Do you trust me?" he whispered back.

"Always."

"I love you, Kyla. I would never hurt you," he reassured. "Can I touch you?"

"Touch me," I murmured.

Tyler's right hand moved to my breast, kneading over my bra, as he held himself up with the other. His mouth moved down to the swell of my breast, placing kisses along the way. He gently pulled the cup of my bra down, exposing my breast and continued to kiss. I arched my back up off the mattress, so he could undo the clasp. He pulled it off, letting my breasts fall free and tossed it to the side. He sat back on his knees and looked down at me. "So beautiful," he whispered.

He lowered down over my right breast, his hand gently squeezing me, as he sucked my nipple into his mouth. Then he moved his attention to the other one. I wrapped my arms around his shoulders, pulling him to me and ran my nails down his back. I closed my eyes and arched up into him, letting out a soft moan. It felt so good having Tyler's mouth on me. Taking what I was

49

so freely giving. The pleasure washed over me, as I felt wetness pool between my legs.

I eased back down to the bed, and I put my hands on his shoulders. Tyler looked up at me questioningly, seeing if I was okay. "Lower," I urged him. I wanted his mouth all over me. Consuming me. He kissed his way down my flat stomach, swirling his tongue over my belly button.

He stopped just above my thong, his eyes never leaving mine. "Yes?" he questioned, checking that I was still with him.

"Yes… please…" I wanted his hands and mouth on my most sensitive parts.

Tyler slowly tucked his fingers into the strings of my thong and gently pulled them down, revealing all of me to him. A low growl erupted from his chest in appreciation of my body. He pulled my thong down my legs and over my ankles, tossing it next to my bra. Kneeling down between my legs, he kissed between my hips and down to my bare pussy. His tongue pushed between my folds as he began to lick me up and down. He swirled his tongue on my clit. I felt the sensation start low in my belly and start to build. He replaced his tongue with his thumb and moved it in small circles on my sensitive nub as his mouth moved lower to my wetness. He slid his tongue in and licked my opening. Ty lapped me up, over and over again. His tongue worked furiously. My hips pushed up to his mouth as I searched for more, letting him know how good this felt. My body was on fire and all conscious thought left my mind. Another strangled moan escaped my lips. The pleasure continued to build.

Pulling back, he ran his hands up the insides up my thighs, gently massaging me. He took two fingers and slipped them into my wetness and began to pump them in and out. The intrusion was delicious and welcomed. I arched my back off the bed, letting noises slip from my lips that I had never made before. "Tyler…. more… oh god… more."

"So beautiful. You feel so good. So wet for me. Come for me, baby."

50

"I can't... I can't," I cried.

"Yes, you can. Let go and come for me." He started pumping harder and wiggled his fingers back and forth, massaging me from the inside. He hit that sweet spot that started me reeling. I arched off the bed and grabbed the sheets in my fists. His tongue went down and brushed over my clit, sucking it into his mouth.

Pressure continued to build, traveling from my core through my body down to my toes. "It's too much... Oh god...Ty." I exploded. The ecstasy washed through my body, consuming me, as I threw my head back and continued to writhe on the bed. The release was amazing as Tyler continued to pump me through my orgasm. I felt my pussy clenching his fingers that were deep inside me.

*Oh my god!*

# Chapter 14
## Tyler

She finally relaxed back onto the mattress, as I eased my fingers from her slick pussy. "That was... amazing," she panted.

I moved up to kiss those lips that had just cried out my name. "That was the most beautiful thing I've ever seen. You coming apart in my hands. I gotta be inside you, baby." As I kissed her, all I could think about was how it would feel to have those lips wrapped around my dick.

Kyla wrapped her arms around my neck. She glowed as she looked up at me. "I love you, Tyler. I want all of you." She bit her lip and looked down at my dick straining to break free from my boxer briefs. I followed her eyes and saw the tip poking out the top. Her tongue ran along her bottom lip. "I want you in my mouth. I want to make you come too."

*Did she really just say that?* I felt myself harden even more at her words. "Baby, you don't have to do that. I don't expect you to."

"I know and that makes me want to even more. I want to make you feel as good as you made me feel."

This girl was my dream. God, I loved her. I sat back on my legs and pulled her up with me. Grabbing her face in my hands, I kissed and kissed her. We became more desperate with each one. My hands rubbed up and down her body, memorizing every curve.

We untangled ourselves as her hands reached down to the top of my boxer briefs. She slowly began to push them down my thighs and I sprang free. My dick was hard and ready. I was afraid I wasn't going to last long at this rate. I lifted myself and helped her slide them the rest of the way, tossing them to the floor.

I laid back on the bed as she got on her knees. God, she was gorgeous! Her tits full and round, nipples hard and on display for me. I reached up to palm one, rolling her nipple between my finger and thumb. She let out a gasp and threw her head back.

She leaned down towards me and kissed my stomach like I had done to her. Her hand reached down and wrapped around my cock, stroking it up and down. God, that felt good! Her tongue poked out and licked my precum, spreading it around the tip of my dick. The anticipation was killing me. Finally, she locked those soft lips around me, and began to move. I watched as her head bobbed up and down, still stroking me with her hand. My dick moving in and out of her mouth was hot as hell.

I winced when her teeth nicked the head of my cock. "No teeth, baby."

She looked at me with wide eyes. "I'm so sorry... I've never done this before."

"I know. It's so good, just be careful with your teeth." I encouraged. She wrapped her lips back around me and continued to move up and down, swirling her tongue around the head. It felt so fucking good! I put my hands on top of her head and pushed her deeper and deeper. So fucking good! I felt the head of my dick hit the back of her throat. I had to stop, or I would choke her.

I reached down and pulled her up to me. Her lips were swollen from being wrapped around my dick. "You gotta stop Ky, or I'm gonna come in your mouth. I really wanna be inside you when I come."

She looked at me with lust filled eyes and laid back down, her hair spilling onto the pillow under her head. Waiting all these months 'til she was ready had been pure torture, but this night was worth it. She was worth it.

I reached over to the nightstand, grabbed the condom and ripped the foil with my teeth. I slowly rolled it down the length of my cock and took a deep breath. This was it. I gently nudged her legs apart with my knees and she opened wider for me. I looked into those green eyes, "I love you, Kyla. Tell me if I hurt you, baby. I don't want to ever hurt you."

"Tyler... I love you too. You won't hurt me."

I pressed my lips to hers then pulled back to look at her one last time. This night was going to change everything about us. I reached down and grabbed my cock, guiding it to her slick pussy. I pushed the tip in, checking to make sure she was still okay. She nodded for me to keep going. I pushed in farther, moving slowly. Fuck she was tight! Her wetness slicked my dick and held tight. I pushed a little further 'til I felt her resistance. I stopped, letting her adjust to me. "This might hurt a little."

"I'm ready. Please... just do it," she begged.

I thrusted my hips into her, until I felt the resistance give away. She jerked underneath me, tensing up. Her eyes squeezed shut and tears rolled down her cheeks. *Shit! What have I done?* "God, Kyla, I'm so sorry. I didn't want to hurt you." I reached up and wiped her tears away with the pad of my thumb.

"I'm okay... just a pinch. It's over," she assured me. "You feel so good inside me. Keep going."

"You sure?"

"I'm sure. Tyler, we've waited so long... just fuck me!" She arched her back and pushed her hips up, taking me deeper.

*Say what? Who is this girl?* When the shock of her words wore off, I started to move in and out of her slowly, savoring the feeling of her wrapped around me. It felt so good. Picking up my pace, sweat started to bead on my chest and head as I thrusted into her over and over again. "So fucking good, baby. Oh my god!"

"More... I need more. Fuck me harder," she cried. She reached her hand between us and started rubbing her clit, making her climb higher. The sight of her touching herself, was pushing me to the brink of insanity. Her back arched off the bed as she threw her head back "I'm gonna come again!"

I felt her pussy grip my dick as she shattered beneath me. I pushed harder going balls deep, as I felt my own release building. So close. Two more thrusts and I fell over the edge with her. I slowed down as I pushed out the last of my orgasm and collapsed on top of her. I pushed up on my elbows, so I wouldn't crush her and looked into her eyes as she smiled up at me looking totally satisfied. "Good?" she smirked.

"Good? Good doesn't start to describe it. Fucking amazing."

# Chapter 15
## Kyla

Tyler pulled out and walked to the bathroom to clean up. I stared at his ass, as he disappeared inside. I flopped back on the bed, throwing my arms out to the sides. *Wow! Just wow!* Tori was so right. That was amazing.

Tyler returned with a warm washcloth for me. He leaned over and gently reached down between my legs. "I can do that," I said feeling a little embarrassed.

"I got you," he insisted. He wiped me clean, rubbing against my tender sex. "Kyla, your bleeding," he said, a tinge of panic in his voice.

"It's okay. I knew I would. Sooo worth it, baby. I wouldn't change a thing." I couldn't seem to wipe the silly grin from my face.

He threw the washcloth on the nightstand and crawled into bed with me, pulling the sheet over us. We laid looking at each other, both on our sides, hands propped up under our heads.

"Who knew?" he asked.

Confusion crossed my face, "What do you mean?"

"What happened to my sweet, quiet girl? You surprised me tonight." He grinned at me.

I felt the red start to creep up my neck and into my cheeks again, thinking about the words that had come from my mouth. I didn't even know I could make some of the sounds that had escaped. Honestly, when I was with Tyler, all thought fled from my brain and my body took over. I couldn't explain it.

"Don't get all shy on me now." He reached out and touched the tip of my nose, then leaned in for a quick kiss. "It was sexy as hell. Underneath all this sweet, lives a little sex kitten."

I dropped down on the bed and pulled the pillow over my head. *He did not just say that!* "Ugh!" I groaned.

Suddenly the pillow was being lifted off my head, and my hair fell into my eyes tangling over my face. Tyler pushed it out of my eyes and lifted my chin up to look at him. "Just gives me one more thing to add to the list of things I love about you," he assured me.

"Would it be crazy to say I want to do it again?" I asked, feeling a little braver.

Tyler flipped me onto my back, hovering over me, smile a mile wide. Dimples front and center. "There she is. My little sex kitten. I'd make love to you a hundred times, if you'd let me."

"Yes, please!" I begged.

Tyler quickly jumped up and went to his bag, coming back with two more condoms. He tore one open, sliding it over himself. He gently slid into me. I ignored the soreness and let the pleasure take over.

We made love well into the morning hours, until we were both so spent that we collapsed with exhaustion. Tyler brought the sheet up over us. Lying behind me, he pulled me in tight so that my head rested just below his chin. He kissed the top of my head and whispered, "I love you," as we drifted off to sleep.

The next morning, I woke to soft kisses along my face, and hands roaming my body. I let out a soft moan, then realization hit. I threw my hand over my mouth and turned away.

Tyler pulled his hand back in surprise, "Babe? What's wrong?"

"Morning breathe," I mumbled through my hand. "Give me a minute?"

Tyler let out a low laugh. "Sure. Do your thing."

I wrapped the sheet around me, stumbled out of bed, grabbed my bag, and headed toward the bathroom. I shut the door and looked in the mirror. *OH, HOLY HELL!* My hair looked like a rat's nest, sticking up all over and I had black smudges under my eyes. I was far from the goddess I had looked like last night.

I grabbed my brush and tried to tame the tangles in my hair. Using some toilet paper, I rubbed at the makeup around my eyes. I quickly brushed my teeth and looked back in the mirror. Okay, not great, but definitely an improvement!

I walked back into the room, still cloaked in the sheet. Tyler scanned me up and down from his place on the bed. "Better?"

"Better." I nodded.

"Good, now come here so I can ravage you some more."

I crawled across the bed to him. "Good morning." I smiled, leaned down, and gave him a deep kiss. *Hmmm?* His mouth was minty fresh. "How long have you been up?"

"A while. I couldn't sleep."

I looked at him questioningly. "Why didn't you wake me?"

"I was thinking about what an amazing night we had and…I like watching you sleep." He tapped the tip of my nose. "You looked so peaceful."

"Stalker much?" I giggled.

"Only you." He grabbed me around the waist and pulled me on top, so I was straddling him. My hair fell in my face and I almost let go of the sheet that was still tightly wrapped around me.

He reached up, gently pulled the sheet from my grasp, and slid it down my body. No longer hidden by the darkness, I felt exposed and self-conscious. He ran his hands up my stomach to cup my breasts. He massaged me gently, rolling my nipples, and effectively getting me out of my own head.

"Sooo beautiful," he hissed. "Ride me?"

"Tyler, I don't know…" I protested. I wasn't sure I could do *that*.

He placed a finger to my lips to quiet my worry. "I think we proved last night that we're good together. We'll figure it out. Together. It's like our bodies were made for each other. I want to share all my firsts with you."

Well, if that didn't melt my heart. I fell a little bit more in love with him at that moment. "Yes. I want that too."

He lifted me up and reached over to the nightstand to grab a condom. I raised up on my knees and lined myself up with him. Tyler placed his hands on my hips as I lowered myself on his length. The feeling was so different, so deliciously good. I sunk lower until there was nothing between Ty and myself. I threw my head back and gasped. I placed my hands on his abs for leverage and slowly lifted my hips only to sink back down.

"Fuck, that's good, Ky." Tyler's eyes rolled back as he arched off the bed. I leaned down to kiss his lips. As I leaned forward, I rubbed my clit against his shaft, sending tingles through me. I slid back and did it again, over and over. I was shamelessly seeking my own pleasure. He pushed up into me, every time I came down, making me feel so full. The sensation between my legs started to grow stronger and stronger, building and building, climbing higher and higher. I rubbed my clit on him one more time and shattered again as wave after wave of bliss consumed me. I collapsed onto Tyler's chest in exhaustion. Gripping my hips harder, he pumped up into me faster and faster until he cried out with his own release.

"Oh, god." I panted into his chest as his arms wrapped around my body and held me tight. "I had no idea that's what we were missing. "

"No shit. That was awesome," he gasped. "Ky, I want to spend every day buried deep inside you. Now that I've had you, I don't want it to end."

"God, I feel the same way. This summer is going to be... I just want to spend every minute with you before we go away to college."

"Shhh! Don't talk about that now. Let's just enjoy the summer."

We were meeting Tori and Chris for breakfast at the corner diner. We could have just met up at the hotel, but I really didn't want to do the walk of shame with an audience.

The awkwardness I thought would be there in the morning, wasn't. "Babe, hurry your beautiful ass up. We have to meet them at 10:30. We're going to be late."

"I'm almost done," I called out. "Just give me a minute."

"I'd give you a thousand minutes, but you know we're already going to have to deal with their *I told you so* bullshit."

"Okay, I'm ready," I said throwing on my jeans and pulling myself together enough to be presentable. We left the hotel room with our heads held high. Hand in hand. We didn't look back or feel ashamed. We were in love.

We walked into the diner and spotted Chris and Tori in the back corner waiting for us. "Well, well, well...look who decided to show," Chris mocked us.

"You said 10:30, it's like 10:35. Give us a break," Tyler shot back.

"I'm just sayin' I wasn't sure you'd make it." Chris was not going to cut us a break.

Tyler slid in and I squeezed into the booth next to Tori and she gave me a quick hug. "How was it?" she whispered in my ear.

"Later." I waved her off, a silent message exchanged between us. She raised her eyebrow in understanding.

We ordered breakfast and ate with easy conversation flowing between the four of us. We relived the night, discussing the typical high school gossip. Funny moments of the night and of course the outrageous. "I can't believe it's over." I sighed. "Our senior year is over!"

"You know what that means, don't you?" Chris looked at the three of us. We looked at each other questioningly, shaking our heads.

"It means our kick-ass summer is about to begin, bitches!" Chris held up his water glass as a toast.

We raised ours in return. "To summer," Tyler toasted. "To summer," we chanted and clinked glasses in a fit of laughter.

I couldn't wipe the happiness from my face, as I looked at my friends. I was so lucky to have these amazing people in my life.

# Chapter 16
## Tyler

Two months. That's all we would have before I had to leave for Michigan State.

After leaving everyone at the diner that morning, I went home to an empty house. I grabbed a few beers out of the fridge, jumped back in my car and drove out to the lake. I sat on a picnic table looking out over the water. Lost in my own thoughts. I turned my hat backward and took another long pull off the bottle in my hand.

When I accepted the football scholarship to MSU back in January, I was excited. That was my dream. I had wanted to play college ball forever. My dad took me to a game when I was ten and that was it for me. I had looked at the stadium full of people, all cheering for their team. The energy was electric. I felt it consume me. I wanted to be running onto that field, earning the screams of the crowd. From that day forward, I lived and breathed football.

Until Kyla.

I wanted to move away from home. Live life in the dorms. Explore the life that awaited me on the MSU campus. The freedom. The girls. The parties. Just break free and be me.

Until Kyla.

I never planned on falling so deeply in love. Never planned on needing someone else like I needed air. Never saw myself planning a future beyond football.

Until Kyla.

I finished off my first beer and twisted the top off another, trying to drown out my own thoughts.

Now I was fucked. The things I wanted then and the things I wanted now weren't in sync. I wanted Kyla every

62

minute of every day. She was beautiful with her long blond waves and bright emerald eyes. Eyes I could get lost in for hours. She looked at me as if she could see my soul.

Touching her last night had been better than anything I could have imagined. She was so responsive. I saw a different side of her last night. I hadn't planned on going down on her, but I had to taste her. I wanted all of her. Knowing I was the only one to ever touch her like that, taste her like that, please her like that, fuck her so thoroughly 'til her body went limp... not gonna lie, knowing I could do that to her, was a turn on in itself. Seeing my sweet girl transform into the sex kitten she was last night was ... there really were no words. I felt myself harden just thinking about her again.

Now I was fucked. Two months and I had to leave for football training. I wouldn't be able to see her every day. Hell, it could be weeks. Training would be intense and would require me to be focused on the game.

Kyla, Tori and Chris were all going to Western. They would all be together, and I was going to be alone. I was following my dreams, not my girl. The campuses were close, but I was going to be so busy that the ninety-minute drive might as well be ninety hours. Maybe Western would be a better choice for me.

I finished off my last beer and dropped the bottles in a trash bin on my way back to the car. I slid in the seat and dropped my head down to the steering wheel. How was I going to do this? Being away from Kyla was going to be torture. Something needed to change.

I needed to see my girl. Needed to talk to her. I grabbed my phone out of my pocket and pushed her number. *Please pickup. Please pick up.*

"Hey, baby," she cooed into my ear.

"Kyla. I need to see you. Can I come over?"

# Chapter 17
## Kyla

That was just weird. I sat on the front steps looking at the black screen of my phone, waiting for Tyler. He sounded disconnected. Was he regretting last night? Had I just made the biggest mistake of my life? Did I just give everything away and he was going to walk away? I couldn't stop the wheels from turning. I thought everything had been perfect, could I have been that naïve?

A few minutes later, Tyler's car pulled up in the driveway. I tentatively stood and waited for him to get out of the car. He had his hat pulled low over his eyes and didn't look up at me as he approached.

This was going to be bad. I could feel it. Tension hung in the air between us. I wrapped his hand in mine and led him to the backyard, where we could talk in private. My stomach was churning with dread at what was about to come. He hadn't said a word. Yet.

We sat on the bench covered in ugly cushions that sat in the corner of the patio. I tucked my leg under me and turned to face him. "Tyler, what's going on?"

He finally lifted his head and stared at me. He looked lost and his sad eyes were rimmed with red. "I can't do this."

I took a deep breath, hoping he wasn't saying what I thought he was saying. "What do mean you can't do this? Have you been drinking?" I knew the answer to my second question, by the stench of beer emanating from him.

"A little," he admitted, turning his hat backwards on his head. "I don't know what I want anymore," he stated matter-of-factly.

This was it. The breakup that I had dreaded. "But I thought you liked it...where we were going."

He put his hands on my cheeks and held my face, then leaned his forehead against mine. "I did. But I can't go there with you and I hate myself for it."

"Did? You changed your mind that fast. What the hell?" Tears welled up in my eyes and a single tear rolled down my cheek. This was unbelievable. I didn't know whether to be raging mad or totally heartbroken. "How could you do this?" I demanded. Raging mad was winning out as I stood and started pacing in front of the stupid bench with the stupid, ugly cushion.

Tyler reached out and grabbed my wrist, turning me towards him. "Kyla, I'm doing this for you. For us."

I yanked my arm back. We had never even had an argument up to this point. I couldn't believe this was happening. God, I was so stupid! "Are you seriously going to sit there and act like you're doing me a favor?"

Tyler stood and grabbed my hands bringing them together at his chest. He stared down at me. "I thought you would be happy about this."

"Happy? Are you serious right now?" The tears flowed down my cheeks now. I turned my back to him. "How could I have been so stupid?" I choked out, full on sobbing now.

He stepped up behind me, wrapping his arms around me tight and pulling me to his chest. My traitorous body fell back against him. I should hate him right now, but I couldn't.

"You're not stupid, babe. You're smart and beautiful. Why would you say that?" He leaned over my shoulder and kissed my neck holding me tenderly.

"Last night..." My throat closed, and I couldn't get it out.

"Was amazing," he whispered in my ear.

I turned and wrapped my arms around his waist. He held me close. One hand was on my lower back the other cupped the back of my head, pressing me to his chest. I peered up at him.

65

"Then why are you doing this? Why are you breaking up with me?"

He grabbed me by the shoulders and turned me to look at him. Tyler stared down at me, his blue eyes wide with recognition. "Kyla, is that what you thought? Oh my God, baby. No! Just…no! He pulled me in again, crushing me to him and wrapping his body tightly around mine. "I'm not breaking up with you, Ky!"

"I'm so confused," I admitted. "You said you couldn't do this. I thought you meant us."

His face quirked up on one side in a half smile. I didn't understand. "I'm so sorry," he apologized. "We need to work on our communication," he continued, pointing back and forth between us. "I meant I couldn't leave you in the fall. I'm so in love with you. I always wanted to go to MSU to play football, but I don't know how I'm going to stand being away from you. I'm thinking of going with you to Western instead. It's just so confusing, because I still want to play ball, but I didn't count on falling in love. I don't know if I can have both, and I choose you."

Relief flooded my body as understanding sunk in. "You thought you had to choose?" I pulled him back over to the ugly cushions on the bench. I sat, pulling him down with me. "You don't have to choose, Tyler. I would never ask you to give up your dreams for me. You can have both."

"Yeah? I don't know how that is going to work. I'll be so busy with practice and classes, there won't be any time left for us," he confessed.

"We'll make time for us. We'll make this work. I'll only be down the road. We can do this," I said.

"It's not going to be easy, Kyla. The team schedule is going to be demanding. I don't want to lose you."

"And I don't want you to ever resent me for keeping you from your dreams. We can do this," I reassured. "Okay?"

"Okay. You're amazing, you know that?" He leaned in close. His tongue ran along my bottom lip before pushing deep inside. His hands tangled in my hair as he pulled me in. His kiss scorched me, burned me from the inside out.

I pulled back. "You know what this means? Since our time will be limited, we will have to take advantage of this summer," I said mischievously.

"Oh yeah…what exactly do you have in mind, baby girl?"

I waggled my eyebrows at him. "A summer we won't forget."

# Chapter 18
## Tyler

Begin "Operation: Kick-Ass Summer". Chris and I were meeting with the girls to start the planning process. The guys wanted to just wing-it. The girls...well, Kyla... insisted we come up with a plan. She said if we didn't plan stuff, pretty soon the summer would be over, and we wouldn't have "maximized our time together". She was a planner. Which is probably how she ended up being the class valedictorian. I loved that she was so smart and put thought into everything she did. If I had been like her, I'm sure I would have ended my senior year with better grades. But she loved me—flaws and all.

We drove out to the beach, windows down, music blaring through the speakers. Now that we had graduated the feeling of freedom was taking over, even if it was only for a couple of months. I was going to enjoy every minute with my girl.

"Sooo...I'm assuming prom night went good," Chris shouted over the radio.

I reached over and turned the volume down. "Yeah," I answered nonchalantly.

"She didn't freak out on you or anything, did she?"

"Nah, man. Just the opposite actually. There's definitely two sides to that girl," I answered smugly, but not giving too much away.

"So, she's a freak in the sheets, huh? Good for you, man." He nodded his approval.

I punched him in the arm. "Dude! She's my girl. Don't talk about her like that. Not cool, man!"

He grabbed his arm in mock hurt, rubbing it up and down. "What? I'm happy for you. Tori's a total freak in bed and

68

I love it. That girl will be the death of me, but what a way to go." Chris leaned back in the seat and let out a contented sigh. "I'm telling you when she goes down…"

"Stop!" I interrupted him mid-sentence. "I get the point. I don't need the details."

"That's cool, man. But if you don't think Tori and Kyla are talking about this same stuff, you're dreaming. Those two…their tight. They're probably talking about our dicks right now."

We pulled up to the lake and walked to the beach where the girls said they would meet us. They were laying on the beach worshiping the sun. I stopped when I saw Kyla in her red bikini with her hair piled on top of her head in a messy knot. Her face was free of make-up and she was even more beautiful. I had to adjust myself and pull my shirt down to hide my growing hard-on.

The girls were talking quietly and giggling like crazy. I loved seeing her this way. Carefree and happy.

"Mind if we join you?" I asked standing above the girls staring down at them.

Tori squinted up at us, using her hand to block out the sun. "Uhh…I don't think so. We have boyfriends."

Kyla opened one eye to look at me. "Yeah," she said. "They're big, bad football players. I wouldn't mess with them if I were you."

Chris crossed his arms over his chest. "I'm sure we can take them. What do these guys look like?"

Tori jumped in. "Oh, you know… tall, big muscles, kind of hot actually," she said with a smirk.

"Hot, huh?" Chris leaned down, scooped Tori up, threw her over his shoulder and started running towards the water. "I'll show you hot, baby!"

"Chris! Don't you dare! Put me down!" Tori screamed as he tossed her into the lake. He followed her into the water splashing and laughing.

I sat down next to Kyla giving her a quick kiss. "Hey, sexy".

"Hey," she said as she grabbed her sunglasses off the towel and placed them on her face.

I had to know. My eyes hiding behind my aviators, I squinted at her and asked, "Were you girls talking about our dicks?"

"Kyla's eyes went wide behind her sunglasses. "What? No! Why would you ask that?" The red creeping into her cheeks gave her away.

"Oh my god! You were, weren't you?" I started laughing so hard I could barely catch my breath. "Chris was so right. You girls are so bad."

"She's my best friend...we just...I'm so embarrassed." She grabbed the hat off my head and pulled it down low on hers, hiding her face.

I lifted the brim, exposing her horrified face. I couldn't stop laughing. "I don't care. Just didn't take you for the type to kiss and tell. I hope it was all good."

She looked up at me. "Very good," she said, smiling.

Chris and Tori started back up the beach toward us, both dripping wet and laughing. Tori wrung her hair out over her shoulder. "Well, that was fun."

"Dude, you were so right," I said, nodding to Chris. "They were totally talking about our dicks."

The expression on Tori's face was priceless as she looked between the two of us. "Told you so," Chris threw back and we collapsed in a fit of laughter.

"You're such an asshole." Tori swatted at Chris.

"That's not what you said last night, 'Oh, Chris, harder, harder. You're so awesome, Chris!'" he imitated Tori, barely able to catch his breath from laughing so hard.

Tori jumped on him, covering his mouth with her hand. He pulled it away. "Oh, Chris!" he moaned, imitating her again.

Tori struggled to use both hands to cover his mouth, sitting on his chest. He held her wrists and pulled her hands from his mouth. "You know you love it."

"I do," she conceded, a ridiculous grin on her face.

By the time we left the beach, we had a pretty extensive list of things we wanted to do during the next two months. Kyla and I had both gotten jobs for the summer. We would need the money in order to fulfill the list we came up with. She was going to be working at the marina and I was helping my uncle with his lawn service. We would be busy during the days, but the nights would be ours together.

We decided that to end the summer, the four of us would go to Tori's family's house on Lake Michigan, just past Traverse City. Her mom and stepdad spent a lot of time there in the summer, but Tori had talked them into letting us use it for a week at the end of July. Kyla's parents weren't too keen on the idea, but she convinced them that she was going away in the fall anyway and they wouldn't know what she would be doing. We were moving into adulthood and making our own decisions.

I had to be at MSU for football training starting the first week of August. Kyla would go back to the marina and work until she left for Western toward the end of August. I was going to try and come home on weekends but couldn't make any promises. The week at the lake house would be our last chance for quality time together for a while. It would be the best and worst week of my life.

# Chapter 19
## Kyla

The summer was flying by. I spent my days catering to the rich people at the marina. I was at their beck and call. They placed orders of beer, booze, food, and ice. I took the orders, filled them and ran them out to the docked boats in the marina. I was a glorified waitress, but the tips were good. Usually my mornings flew by, as people prepared to take their boats out on Lake St. Clair.

By my second week on the job, I knew most of the regulars and they treated me well. Some of the older guys were a little over friendly, but I didn't mind. It was harmless flirting, and the payout in tips was worth it.

Tyler's uncle had gotten the contract at the marina, so once a week I would get to see him. He looked sexy in his work clothes. The sleeveless shirt showed off his muscular arms. Paired with the shorts and work boots, he was pure sex. And of course, his hat, always backwards, the way I liked it. I looked forward to the times I could drink him in and be thankful that he was mine.

Today was one of those days. I walked toward the main building after making a delivery at the end of the marina. I was in my own little world, thinking about Tyler, when one of the bigger boats started pulling into the slip ahead of me. I raised my hand to my eyes, blocking the sun, to get a better look. Usually, Mr. and Mrs. Murphy were on this boat, but today their prick of a son, Derick, was on it with a group of rowdy guys. They were loud and obnoxious, and I could see that the boat was littered with empty bottles.

"Just my luck," I muttered to myself as I tried to walk by unnoticed.

"Hey, boat girl," he yelled out. I pretended not to hear him and kept walking. "I'm talking to you, boat bitch!"

I stopped in my tracks. *Seriously?* I turned and faced him, arms crossed. "Are you talking to me?" I asked, narrowing my eyes at him.

"Yeah, I'm talking to you. You're here to serve us and we need service. Bring your pretty little ass over here and take our order," he slurred out.

Jeez, it was only two in the afternoon and these guys were wasted already. I dealt with drunk people every day, but none had disrespected me like this before. I put my hands on my hips and plastered on a fake smile. "If you'd like to place an order, just call the main building and someone will bring it out to you." I turned to walk away but heard him jump off the boat and onto the dock.

He walked over to me, standing a little too close for my comfort. Towering over me, he looked down at me. His hand came around my back and palmed my ass. "I don't want to call it in. You're here now, and I want you to take my order."

I turned out of his groping hands and took a step back. I looked from him to the other guys on the boat. They seemed to be enjoying the show, cheering Derick on. Mustering all the confidence I could at just five-foot tall, I reminded him, "That's not really the way it works here. You'll have to call it in or go up to the main building yourself." I turned to walk away but didn't get far.

"I don't think so." He grabbed my arm hard, fingers biting into my skin, and yanked me hard toward the boat. I lost my balance and fell forward onto my hands and knees. Pain tore through my knee where it had been ripped open by one of the screws on the dock. Blood gushed down my shin from the gash.

I fell on my side, looking around me in a daze, for a way to escape. By now, our scene had started to attract attention from the other boaters. People were whispering to each other, but no one stepped in to help. I saw the marina owner running towards us, with security. Someone must have called it in. I silently begged him to hurry. Derick seemed oblivious to what was going on around us, his focus was solely on me.

He squeezed my arm tighter and yanked me back to my feet. He got right in my face and groped at my breast. "Get up, sweetheart! Come on the boat with us. I promise we'll show you a good time." The sneer in his voice combined with the alcohol on his breath offended my senses and made me cringe. *This was not happening*! He was yanking me toward the boat. "Stop! No!" I yelled, trying to pull away. He was too strong and squeezed harder, pulling me into his body. I yelped out as the pain shot down my arm. I dug my heels in, trying to keep him from getting me on that boat.

"Let her go!" I heard Tyler's angry voice behind me. I turned to look, pleading for him to help me.

The drunk prick stood his ground, and never released his grip on me. "I'm just trying to place my order. Mind your own business, asshole."

"She IS my business, fucker!" I saw Tyler's arm cock back and his fist smashed into Derick's face. Derick's grasp on my arm immediately released as he fell to the ground with one punch. Tyler leaned down toward his crumpled body and spewed venom, "Learn some fucking manners, asshole".

I was shaking so badly that my legs couldn't hold me, and I collapsed to the dock. Tyler reached down and scooped me up, one arm behind my back and the other under my legs. I wrapped my arms around his neck, buried my face in his chest and sobbed softly as he carried me toward the building. "Shhh. I got you, baby." His voice soothed my nerves. From the corner of my eye, I saw security dragging Derick Murphy and his friends out of the marina. Relief washed over me. I felt safe in Tyler's strong arms. I knew he wouldn't let anything else happen to me.

Once inside, Tyler took me to the employee breakroom, and sat down on the old, vinyl couch. He held me tight, as I tried to pull it together. "It's okay, Ky. I got you," he whispered to me, as he gently smoothed my hair back out of my face and kissed my forehead.

I don't know how long I sat there in Tyler's arms, shaking, as I clung tightly to his warmth and security. A few minutes later, or maybe longer, I'm not sure, Mr. Olsen, the marina owner, came to check on me. He kneeled down next to the couch. "Kyla, I'm so sorry that happened to you. I came as fast as I could. Derick Murphy won't be bothering you anymore. I've banned him and his friends from the marina. I'll be calling Mr. and Mrs. Murphy to let them know what happened here today."

I nodded my acknowledgement of his words. "Thank you, Mr. Olsen. I should have...should have just taken his damn order. I know the Murphy's are important members."

Mr. Olsen looked at me with sympathy, shaking his head. "That may be, but I won't tolerate that type of treatment toward my employees. This is not your fault. I know the Murphy's won't be happy when they hear what their son pulled today. I'm just glad Tyler was there to help you. That should have never happened." He turned to Tyler. "Let's get her cleaned up and then I want you to take her home. I'll call your uncle and explain what happened. I'm sure he can have someone come pick up your work truck."

"Thank you, sir. I'm sorry I punched him. I just got so pissed when I saw his hands on Kyla. I kind of lost control."

Mr. Olsen waved Tyler off. "Are you kidding me? Derick Murphy is a spoiled little prick. That punch to his face was long overdue."

# Chapter 20
## Tyler

While Kyla was getting her knee bandaged, I made a quick call to Chris. I gave him the short version of what had happened and asked him to pick me up at Kyla's house, since I was leaving the truck at the marina. Being the good guy he was, he agreed without hesitation.

Just as I ended the call, Kyla hobbled over to me. "You probably need stitches in that knee. You shouldn't be walking on it," I said.

"I don't need stitches. They just put some butterfly bandages on it. I can walk fine." She winced.

"Yeah? I don't think so." I shook my head.

Kyla rolled her eyes at me. "It's fine, really."

"It's not fine," I said as I scooped her up. I carried her out to her car. She insisted she could walk, but fuck that! I didn't want her walking on it right away. I planned on taking care of my girl.

I placed her in the passenger seat of her car, took the keys and slipped into the driver's side. "Let me see your arm." I lifted her left arm to look at it. It was still red and starting to bruise. I could see the outline of that asshole's fingers where he grabbed her. "How bad does it hurt?" I asked, trying to hide my anger.

"It's just a little sore," she answered rubbing her hand over the dark marks on her arm. "It'll be okay." She looked at me with her glistening green eyes. I could see the tears that were about to fall. "Thank you for taking care of me today."

"When I pulled up, I came to find you to say 'hi'. When I saw that guy's hands on you, I just…I saw red. I ran to you as fast as I could. I'm just sorry I didn't get there sooner. I've never

76

punched someone before, but I don't regret it. I'd do it again. Always… for you."

"I was scared," she admitted.

"I know, baby." I threaded my fingers through hers and brought them to my lips, kissing her hand. "Let's go home."

The ride home was quiet. I held her hand as she leaned against the window and stared off into the distance. I'm sure she was replaying what had happened.

So was I. I couldn't keep the murderous thoughts out of my mind. The rage I had felt when I saw him touch her, started to return. I had wanted to rip that guy's head off. I didn't even want to think about what would have happened if he had gotten her on that boat. Nobody touched my girl like that!

I tried to reel it in, as we pulled up in front of her house and I parked the car. Burying my anger, I got out and went around to open her door. I leaned down in front of her. "Here, get on. I'll give you a piggyback." She cracked the first smile I'd seen from her today and climbed up. She wrapped her legs around my waist, draped her arms over my shoulders, and laid her head against my back. I carried her up the walkway to the house.

As we approached, her parents opened the door for us, as I carried her inside. Her mom's hands flew up in front of her face, "Oh my god, Kyla, are you okay? Mr. Olsen called and told us what happened."

"I'm okay. Just shaken a bit."

I looked at Mr. O'Malley. "I'd like to take her up to her room if that's all right, sir."

He nodded his approval, and I took her up the stairs to her room. I carried her to the bed, turned and squatted down so she could climb off my back. I turned and kneeled down between her legs and held her face in my hands. I looked into her sad eyes. "I want you to try to rest. I'm going to go home to take a shower, then I'll come back and maybe we can watch a movie or something."

77

"That sounds perfect," she said. "How'd I get so lucky to have you?"

"Oh, I think you have that backward, sweet girl. I'm the one who's lucky." I gave her a gentle kiss. "I better get back downstairs before your dad comes up here to hunt me down. See you in a bit."

I left her room and headed down the stairs. Mr. O'Malley stood at the bottom waiting for me. "Thank you for what you did for my daughter today. You've earned my respect, son." He reached out and shook my hand.

"No thanks are necessary, sir. I love her. I'd do anything to protect Kyla. I'm just sorry I didn't get there sooner. I apologize for losing my cool and punching that asshole...excuse my language... in the face."

"From what Mr. Olsen said, 'asshole' sounds about right. I'm glad you took him out." He glanced up the stairs to Kyla's room, concern on his face. "Honestly, how is she?"

I let out a sigh. "Shaken, but not broken. Her arm is going to be bruised pretty badly where he grabbed it and her knee has a big gash. I think she's scared more than anything."

"You did good today. Are you coming back?" Mr. O'Malley stuck his hands into his pockets and looked back at the stairs. "I'd like to think that she needs me, but I think she needs you more tonight."

"I am. I'm going to go take a shower, pick up a pizza and a movie. I should be back in about an hour or so. If that's a all right?"

Mr. O'Malley nodded again. "Do you need a ride home?"

"No, sir. Chris is on his way to pick me up."

"We'll see you later then....and Tyler, again, thank you." He turned and walked away.

I left and ran out to Chris' car that was waiting for me. When I got in, the anger I had been holding back boiled over. "GODDAMN MOTHERFUCKING FUCKER!"

# Chapter 21
## Kyla

That night I slept restlessly. I dreamt about Derick Murphy's hands on me. In my dream—no, nightmare—his hands were all over me, touching me in places I had only let Tyler touch. His words echoed in my head. *Get up, sweetheart! I promise we'll show you a good time.* I struggled to get away, but I couldn't. He just kept pawing at me, grabbing me, violating me.

I startled awake, gasping and sweating. It wasn't real, but I couldn't shake the creepy feeling snaking up my back. I felt dirty. I needed to wash it away.

I made my way to the shower, stripped off my clothes, unwrapped my knee, and stepped into the scalding water. I let it rush over my body as I scrubbed everything away, and let it wash down the drain. I looked at my arm, the black marks in the shape of his hand, were a cruel reminder of the day. I scrubbed at them harder, until the skin was red and raw, but they wouldn't come off. The cut on my knee had opened up again, and the blood trickled down my leg. I leaned against the cold tile and slid down the wall, sobbing into my hands, releasing the sadness and fear inside me.

If it hadn't been for Tyler, it could have been so much worse. I don't know how long I sat there letting the heat soothe me. When the shower ran cold, I turned off the water, put a couple of butterfly bandages back on my knee and got dressed. I crept back to my room and picked up my phone. I looked at the clock…2:14am. It didn't matter, I needed him.

**Ky: R U up?**

It didn't take long for my phone to buzz.

**Ty: Yeah. Can't sleep.**

*Ky: Me neither. Can I call U?*

*Ty: Always*

I needed to hear his voice. He picked up on the first ring. "Hey, baby." His voice calmed me.

"Hey." I searched for the words I needed to say. "I'm sorry about today. I know you're upset. I could see it in your eyes."

"Don't you dare apologize. Kyla, I'm not upset with you. I was pissed because that ass had his hands on you, and I couldn't get to you. I should have been there."

"You were," I assured him. "But it keeps running through my mind."

"Mine, too," he confessed.

"Tyler...I need you," I rasped out.

"I'm on my way."

# Chapter 22
## Tyler

I parked down the street, careful not to wake her parents. As I jogged up to the house, I saw her sitting on the porch, waiting in the shadows. She walked toward me, her bare feet silent on the pavement. Her shorts barely covered her ass and her tight tank was wet from her hair, making her nipples poke through the thin fabric. Every curve of her body was on display for me. She took my hands, not saying a word, and led me around the side of the house.

When we got to the dark corner, she pushed me against the wall. She took my hands and placed them on her tits. Looking up at me through her lashes, she pleaded, "Touch me, Tyler. Please…touch me."

I cupped her tits, lightly rolling her nipples through the fabric. I moved my hands down her curves to her waist and reached around to grab her ass. I pulled her close, so she could feel my hardness against her stomach. She leaned her head back, letting out a soft moan. Kissing up the side of her face, I ran my tongue along the shell of her ear. "What do you need, baby?"

"I need you to take it away. Make me forget," she begged.

"I'll take it away, Ky. I'll make you forget," I promised. She was using me, and I would let her. I would be whatever she needed tonight. Always.

She captured my lips with hers and became needy with lust. Our tongues were frantic to taste each other, consume each other. She reached down and took my hand, placing it at the top of her tank. I pulled down the fabric, freeing her. I rubbed my fingers over her taut nipple, gently rolling the peak. She grabbed my head, pulling at my hair and leaned back. She pushed my mouth to her tits. I took one in my mouth, sucking and teasing her nipple with my tongue. Then uncovered her other glorious tit and gave it the same attention.

My hands ran down her sides 'til they reached the bottom of her shorts. I slipped them up inside, palming her ass and pulling her to me. I rubbed my hardness against her softness. So perfect. I needed her as much as she needed me. Our kissing became desperate as I swallowed her moans. Our tongues tangled. Our pulses quickened. Her hands ran through my hair. I pushed the bottom of her shorts aside and moved my hand toward her heat. I ran my fingers along her entrance and hissed. So wet. So perfect. "You're soaked. So wet for me."

"Please… please," was all she could get out before I slipped two fingers inside her wetness. I pumped them in and out, slow and deep. She was needy and panting, her short breaths ragged. She pushed her hips into my hand, trying to increase the pressure. Her fingernails dug into my back to pull me closer. I followed her lead and increased my speed, curling my fingers inside, pumping her hard. Her legs became jello, as she fell onto my hand. I held her up with one arm wrapped around her waist. "Please, Tyler… fuck me… fuck me… please." A tear ran down her cheek. "Take it all away. Love me."

She unbuttoned my shorts and her hand slid down the front. Taking my cock in her delicate hand, she gripped me tightly and stroked me up and down, rubbing my precum around the head with her thumb. I closed my eyes and basked in the pleasure she was providing. She was relentless in her movements. A low growl escaped my chest. I felt my dick hardening more in her hand, becoming almost painful. "You gotta stop." I grabbed her wrist, pulling her from my shorts.

I reached in my back pocket and took a condom from my wallet. I slid it over my length, then pushing her shorts aside. I bent my knees and lined up with her swollen entrance. I held the back of her thighs as I pushed up into her, lifting her from the ground. She wrapped her legs around my waist and gripped me over the shoulders, holding the back of my head in her hands. I adjusted my hands under her ass and lifted her up off my dick and let her slide back down it. She felt tight like this, clenching me with her slick walls. This girl was pure torture and ecstasy. I continued to pump into her slow and steady, but I needed more leverage. She just needed… more.

I placed one hand on the wall behind me for support and eased down the wall while still inside her. Once I got to the ground, I pulled my shirt up over my head and placed it next to me. "Put your knee on my shirt," I said. She unwrapped her legs from around my waist, as I lifted her up off me. I instantly felt the need to be back inside her. She straddled me, using my shirt to cushion her injured knee, and slid back down on my cock. She put her hands on my shoulders, using them to help push herself up. My hands went to her hips, lifting and guiding her up and down on my dick… faster and harder. It was a torturous pace we were setting, both of us covered in sweat. Her skin glistened in the moonlight.

One of her hands came off my shoulder and slipped down the front of her shorts. She started to rub herself, searching for her release. Her hand moved swiftly, rubbing circles against her clit. I wished we were naked, so I could watch her touch herself. She was so damn sexy, as she threw her head back in wild abandon.

I felt her walls begin to clench around me in wave after wave, as she came hard around my dick. She leaned forward and bit my shoulder, stifling her screams, as she rode out her orgasm. I pumped harder, desperate now, sliding her up and down my cock… faster and faster. I felt the pressure build, taking me closer and closer until I exploded inside her. She pressed her hips into me, taking me all and pushing out the last of my orgasm.

I leaned back against the wall as she collapsed on top of me. Her head rested on my shoulder, as my hand made lazy circles on her back. We were both breathing hard, trying to catch our breath. We sat there in silence, basking in the afterglow of what we had just done—fucked in desperation, in the dark, on the side of her parents' house.

"I used you," she whispered into the night.

"I know."

# Chapter 23
## Kyla

I slept late the next morning, feeling sated and content. I woke to the sunlight streaming through the blinds, catching me in the eye. I rolled over and sighed, replaying last night in my mind. I used Tyler to forget. I should have felt bad, but I didn't.

My phone buzzed on the nightstand next to my bed. I reached my hand over, aimlessly searching for my phone. I finally felt it under my fingertips and pulled it to my face to look at the screen. I smiled when I saw Ty's face lit up.

I answered the call and pulled the phone to my ear, my voice raspy, "Good morning."

"Good morning, beautiful. How'd you sleep?"

"Like a baby. Thank you for last night."

"Anytime," he chuckled. "How are you feeling today?"

"Much better," I answered honestly.

"You up for a party tonight?" he asked. "Cole is having a big Fourth of July blow out tonight. Sounds like everyone's going to be there."

"It might be just what I need."

"I thought I was just what you need," he teased me.

"You are, Ty. Always." And he was.

"Pick you up at six?"

"I'll be waiting."

I called Tori. She and Chris were going to Cole's tonight too. I was excited about the party. It would really be the last time that everyone from school would be together before we all went our separate ways in the fall. I knew my time with Tyler this summer was coming to an end, and I wanted to enjoy every minute I could with him.

I spent a little extra time getting ready. I had been such a wreck yesterday, I wanted to look pulled together. I left my hair down and kept my makeup light. With my deep tan, I really didn't need much. I threw on a pair of jean shorts and a sparkly, black tank top. The bruises on my arm showed, but it was too hot to wear long sleeves. I grabbed a lightweight zip-up before walking out the door. If I started to feel self-conscious, I could cover the bruises with it.

I saw Tyler pull up and ran out to him as he was getting out of the car. I leapt into his arms and wrapped my legs around his waist, catching him off guard. Crashing my lips to his, I kissed him deeply. He spun me around, as I laughed like a giddy girl.

"What's got into you?" He smiled down at me, holding me tight in his arms.

"I just love you so much and I want us to have some fun tonight." I smiled back at him, barely containing my excitement.

"Well, that is the plan." He set me back down on my feet. "Let's go!"

We hopped into his Challenger and sped off toward the party. The windows were down, and I let the wind rush through my hair. I slipped off my sandals and put my feet up on the dashboard. I turned up the radio and leaned back against seat, closing my eyes. Lady Antebellum's "Need You Now" blared through the speakers. I wasn't a big country fan, but something about this song called to me. It reminded me of how I had needed Tyler last night and he had been all too willing to oblige. Before I realized it, I was singing along with the song, pouring all my feeling for him into the words- *It's quarter after one, I'm all alone and I need you now. Said I wouldn't call, but I lost all control and I need you now. And I don't know how I can do without. I just need you now...* I kept singing 'til the song ended, belting out the lyrics, lost in my own head.

When I opened my eyes, Tyler was staring at me, making me feel awkward about singing out loud.

"What? Why are you looking at me like that?" I questioned, feeling the blush creep into my cheeks.

"I've just never heard you sing before." He smiled that panty dropping smile. "That was sexy as hell!"

"Yeah, well it's usually just an in-the-shower thing." I rolled my eyes.

"Well, showering together just became number one on my priority list this summer." By the way he was eye-fucking me, I knew he wasn't kidding.

"Is that so?" I smiled coyly at him. "Another night Romeo. We have a party to go to tonight."

"That, we do, baby girl!"

We pulled up to Cole's house a few minutes later. There were already a lot of people there and we had to park down the street. As we walked into the backyard, hand in hand, we could see that Cole had pulled out all the stops for this party. His house backed up to a private lake, and a bonfire was already burning on the beach. Tables of food and drinks were lined up on the patio and a DJ was set up on the upper deck.

Cole approached us. "Hey, guys. Glad you could make it." Tyler and Cole did that man handshake guy-hug thing. "Kyla, you're looking beautiful, as always."

"Thanks, Cole. This is really amazing!" I said.

"Yeah, my parents are cool. They're in Chicago for the weekend. Drinks are in the cooler. Help yourself."

"Cool, man. Thanks!" Tyler answered.

"No problem. Have fun." Cole turned away to talk to another group of people walking in.

Neither Tyler nor I were big drinkers, but we headed over towards the coolers anyway. Tyler popped the top. "What do you want, babe?" he asked me, pulling out a beer for himself.

I looked at him skeptically. "Don't worry. I'm gonna keep it cool. I have precious cargo to drive home, but I want you to have a good time. I think you deserve it. Besides, maybe I'll get lucky later." He waggled his eyebrows at me.

"Maybe, you will," I flirted with him. "I'll just have a wine cooler."

He opened the bottle and handed it to me. I took a long drink and the berry flavor washed over my tongue. God, that tasted good.

Tyler went over to talk to some of the guys from the team and I found Tori with some of the girls from the cheer squad.

"Hey, girl!" Tori pulled me in for a tight hug. "I heard Tyler knocked some guy out at the marina yesterday, saving your honor. That's soooo romantic!"

"Yeah, he did. But I'm actually trying to forget about it," I said, as I held my drink up.

"Finally! 'Bout time you decided to cut loose. I'm so proud of you," she teased me.

"Couple more of these and I won't care anymore," I said, draining the bottle in my hand.

My second drink went down smoother than the first. Before I knew it, I was on my fourth, and we were shaking our asses to the music the DJ was pumping out. I was a little tipsy and feeling good. Most everyone had moved down to the beach by the bonfire, so Tori and I headed down there too. Everyone was drinking and dancing on the beach, enjoying what was probably our last time together.

I found Tyler sitting in a beach chair by the fire. The flames from the fire illuminated his face and made him look even sexier than he already was. Standing there, I took him in. His blue eyes sparkled in the flames. The music was thumping, and people danced all around us.

The song switched to Rihanna's "Where Have You Been". When Tyler turned and saw me standing there, I saw the lust in his eyes. Heat pooled low in my belly and I suddenly felt frisky. Without breaking eye contact, I downed the rest of my drink and handed the bottle to Tori.

"You go girl!" she encouraged.

I looked him in the eyes and walked toward him. I swiveled my hips, digging my toes into the sand. When I was finally in front of him, I reached down and fisted the front of his shirt. Kissing him deeply, I pulled him to his feet. Releasing the kiss, I kept staring into his eyes, hypnotizing him. I started walking backward, beckoning him to me with the tips of my fingers.

He willingly followed and placed his hands on my hips. The beat picked up and I raised my hands up over my head and started rocking into him. My hips found the rhythm of the music and I let it take over. My hands went to his shoulders and his hands slipped down to cup my ass. I shamelessly ground myself into him. I felt the bulge in his shorts rub against my heat and I lost it. I started swinging my hips back and forth, teasing him, slowly lowering to the ground, raking my nails down his chest 'til I was crouching down in front of him. I pushed back up, rubbing my breasts along his body as I went, my hands skimming along his legs and back to his hips.

Tyler quickly turned me, so that my back pressed up against his chest. His arms went around my waist, pulling my ass into his hard on. We rocked together, forgetting everything and everyone else. I reached up to clasp my arms around his neck, closed my eyes and leaned my head back into his shoulder. We danced as if our two bodies were one. We were on fire with want. Need. Lust. The slight buzz I had, erased all my inhibitions.

Tyler leaned down and whispered in my ear. "You ready to get out of here, baby?"

"God, yes! But don't you want to stay for the fireworks?" I questioned softly.

"Oh, there will be fireworks. I promise you."

# Chapter 24
## Tyler

I held Kyla's hand tight, as we practically ran down the street to where my car was parked. I pressed her up against the car and devoured her lips, kissing her hungrily. When we finally came up for air, I opened the door for her and she slipped in. I moved to the driver's side and started the engine. The look in her eyes told me everything I needed to know.

I punched the gas and headed back to my house. "Where are we going?" she asked.

"My parents are at the casino for the night. They went downtown to see the fireworks and won't be home 'til the morning."

"Perfect," she moaned. She leaned close, reaching over to touch my leg. Her hand crept higher, 'til she was rubbing my hard-on. I loved this side of her. Most of the time she was quiet and reserved, but when it came to sex, all bets were off. It was like she flipped a switch, going from sweet to sexy in a matter of seconds.

"You're killing me, baby," I growled into her hair. My hand moved to the hem of her shorts and I ran my finger up under it. I skimmed along her thigh until I reached her wetness. I loved how she was always so ready for me.

"Drive faster," she ordered, her voice breathless. "I can't wait much longer. I want you so bad."

I took the next turn a little too fast, speeding toward our destination. The short drive seemed to last forever, as she teased me, pulling my zipper down, and reaching inside. Concentrating on driving had never been such a challenge. With her hand on my dick, it took every bit of self-control to keep from swerving. We pulled up to the house and were out of the car in a flash.

I took her hand and pulled her along the sidewalk, through the door, and up to my room. Slamming the door shut behind us, I pushed her up against it. She reached down, grabbed the hem of her tank, lifted it up over her head, and threw it to the floor. I scooped her up in my arms, and her legs wrapped tightly around my waist. I pushed her back against the door and ravished her mouth. We were a mess of tongues and teeth and lips. I loved this girl with all my heart. She was my undoing.

I carried her to the bed and set her on the edge. She was already unbuttoning her shorts and I helped her pull them off, throwing them over my shoulder. I scanned her body, still in her black bra and panties, from her long silky hair down to her pink painted toes. "You are so beautiful, Kyla. I can't get enough of you. You have no idea what you do to me."

Reaching forward, she rubbed her hands along the front of my shorts. "I think I have an idea, but you're wearing too many clothes."

I quickly toed-off my shoes and pulled my shirt up over my head. She was already working on my shorts, undoing the button and zipper. I pushed them down my hips and stepped out of them. There was no hiding how turned on I was, the tent in my boxer briefs left no question.

I kneeled down in front of her and caressed her thighs up to her hips. I tucked my fingers under the material and gently pulled her panties down her legs and off. I pushed her knees apart and gazed at her perfect pussy. Her wetness glistened, showing me just how much she wanted me. I leaned in for a taste and licked through her folds. "So perfect, baby." I poked my tongue into her heat, exploring and devouring her wetness and rubbing it over her clit. She moaned in pleasure, putting her hands on my head and pushing me into her center. I sucked her clit into my mouth, my tongue sweeping across her most sensitive part.

She fell back on the bed and pushed her hips up into my face. I lifted her leg up over my shoulder and continued my

91

assault of her pussy. "Tyler," she moaned. "Finger fuck me…please." I slipped two fingers into her wetness and started pumping them in and out of her. Hooking them inside her, I searched for that spot that made her go crazy. "Oh, god! Oh, god!" she screamed. I added another finger, stretching her further, and sucked her clit hard. That was all it took to push her over the edge, her back arched up off the mattress and she screamed my name. I felt her pussy clenching around my fingers as I pumped her through her orgasm. I would never tire of watching her fall apart from my touch. She was exquisite.

I placed my knee on the mattress and crawled up her body, pulling her further onto the bed. I placed my hands beside her head and stared down at her. I took her arms and placed them up over her head, locking her wrists with my hand. "Open your eyes. I want to see you when you taste yourself." She obeyed, as I leaned down and powerfully kissed her, sticking my tongue deep into her mouth. Her tongue twisted with mine, frantically. "Do you taste that? Do you taste yourself on my tongue?" She slowly nodded her head. "So good."

I reached down and pulled the cups of her bra down, exposing her tits. I sucked one into my mouth, running my tongue across her hard nipple, and rolled the other between my finger and thumb. "Harder," she moaned.

"I don't want to hurt you, Ky."

"You won't. You could never hurt me. Suck harder."

Her wish was my command as I sucked her tit harder into my mouth, pulling and gently biting. I moved to the other one and sucked it hard. She moaned louder and arched off the bed. I slipped my hands behind her back to undo the clasp of her bra. I slid it down her arms and threw it with the rest of our discarded clothes. I rubbed both her tits, filling my hands with her beauty. "So perfect. So beautiful. I gotta be inside you. Now!"

"Take me, Ty. I want to feel you deep inside me. Please…"

Her words were my undoing. I reached to the nightstand and took a condom out of the drawer. I slid my boxer briefs off and slipped it over my hardened cock. I pushed her legs further apart and eased into her pussy. I pushed in slowly, savoring the feeling of her tightness gripping me. "You're so tight, baby. You feel so good." I eased back out and pushed in, harder this time. I wanted her to feel every inch of me. I hovered over her, keeping my weight on my hands, so I wouldn't crush her tiny body.

She wrapped her legs around me, locking her ankles behind my back. It shifted her angle and made it that much better. I picked up my pace, pushing into her over and over. She gripped my shoulders and dug her nails into my back. She bent her neck back and closed her eyes. "Oh, god... That feels so good," she rasped out. She pushed her hips up into mine and began gyrating against my dick, pushing me deeper. She was searching for another release and I would give it to her. I thrust harder and harder, as she pushed up into me again and again. "I'm so... so close, Ty."

"Me too, baby. Come with me. Come with me, Kyla!" My words pushed her over the edge again, screaming out in pleasure. She shattered beneath me, as she held on tight around my neck. I felt her pussy pulsing around my dick in wave after wave of ecstasy. Two more thrusts and I was releasing everything I had into her. I threw my head back, buried myself deep inside her and rode out the high, pushing deeper and deeper. It was the most intense orgasm I'd ever had. I finally collapsed on top her in exhaustion and quickly rolled to the side. "That was... there are no words," I panted into her hair.

"Intense? Awesome? Amazing?" she supplied.

"Yes, to all of it." I answered her. I raised up on one elbow, looked deep into her emerald eyes and bared my heart to her. "I can't explain how I feel about you. The word 'love' doesn't seem to be enough. It's so much more than that," I whispered softly as I twisted her long locks around my finger.

"I know what you mean," she assured me. "I feel the same way. It's like when were apart, a piece of my soul is missing and I'm not complete unless I'm with you."

"Exactly. Now that I've found you, I can't imagine my life without you. It would destroy me," I confessed into the dark.

"It would destroy me too. I think we were destined to be together. Always." She whispered.

"Always."

# Chapter 25
## Kyla

The next day, I met Tori for lunch. We'd been best friends forever, but since Tyler and I had gotten together, we just didn't see each other like we used to. I was in serious need of some girl-time.

I walked into the café a few minutes before noon. Tori was already seated and waving at me frantically.

I threw my purse on the empty chair. "I saw you. You didn't have to flag me down like you were hailing a cab." I laughed, giving her a big hug.

"I haven't seen you in so long. I thought maybe you'd forgotten what I looked like," she teased.

I rolled my eyes. "Don't be so over dramatic. I just saw you last night."

"True," she said. "But it's been like two weeks since we've really had a chance to talk. What's going on with you? Chris told me about what happened at the marina. I know you didn't want to talk about it last night. But what happened?" Concern filled her voice.

Just then the waitress came to take our order, giving me chance to stall. When she walked away, Tori raised her eyebrow questioningly.

I looked down at my hands. "Honestly, it was scary. One of the member's son had too much to drink out on the water. When he came back to the marina, he was totally plastered. He grabbed my arm and tried to haul me onto his boat." I paused, remembering the crazy look in his eyes and rubbed my arm where his hands had bruised me.

"Did he hurt you?" she asked.

95

I showed her my arm. "Just this and my knee. I got a gash from falling onto the dock, but it's healing. His groping hands were the worst. The way he touched me, creeped me out."

"And?" Tori probed.

"And I was scared. And then Tyler showed up out of nowhere. He clocked the guy in the face, and he went down. End of story." I sighed.

"Our Tyler? I have to be honest, I really never thought he had it in him. I've never seen him be aggressive," she said.

"He was like my knight in shining armor. He took care of me all night long." I gave her a sideways glance. "Then he came back later and REALLY took care of me. If you know what I mean...?"

"Oh my god," she squealed. "Did he fuck you that night?"

I threw my hand over her mouth and looked around to see if she had attracted any attention. I looked back at her. "Yes!" I said definitively. "And it was soooo good. And last night. Even better!" I giggled.

She pulled my hand from her mouth. "Who are you? Not even six months ago, I was trying to convince you to let him in, and now you're like some...some sex maniac!"

I rolled my eyes at her again. "I swear you have a flair for drama. I'm not a sex maniac," I assured her. "It's just that when I'm with him, nothing else seems to matter."

"You totally love him, don't you?"

"Yeah, I do," I confided. "I know that this sounds silly, but he is my everything. I can't imagine life without him. I don't know how to explain it."

"You don't have to. I get it. I'm that way with Chris. So.... how is the sex?" she said, leaning close and whispering. "Does he make you..." She spoke even quieter, "does he make you come?"

"Yeah," I said dreamily. "Every. Single. Time. At least twice."

She squealed again, clapping her hands in excitement. "I am so happy for you!"

"I know. I am happy. But do you think it can really last? He's leaving in less than a month. I don't know how I'm going to survive it. What if he gets to MSU and forgets about me?" I worried.

"He's not going to forget about you. He's as in love with you, as you are with him," she assured me.

"I'm so used to seeing him every day." I sighed. "It's going to be hard."

It's called Skype sex, honey. I'm pretty sure it's why Skype was invented."

"Oh…I can't do that. Seriously? That would be totally embarrassing." I cringed at the idea.

"Trust me! Have I ever steered you wrong? Chris and I have done it. Sure, it was awkward at first, but it's totally erotic. Knowing you can see, but you can't touch. It's my personal 3am porno pleasure." She giggled so hard that she snorted.

I swear when Tori and I got together it was always a good time. She could make me laugh like no one else. She was good for the soul and truly the best friend anyone could ever ask for. "You're sick. You know that?"

"Yeah, but you love me anyway!"

"I do. You're the best!"

Tori and I finished our lunch and made plans for later in the week. Tyler's uncle had agreed to let us take his boat out on Wednesday night. I knew Tyler wouldn't mind the extra company. The four of us really hadn't spent that much time together this summer, and it was long overdue.

Wednesday, late afternoon, Tyler, Chris, and Tori met me at the marina. We carried everything we would need onto his uncle's speedboat. It was an inboard cabin cruiser with a sun deck. Awesome for laying out and getting laid. Not that there would be much of the latter, since we had company. But a girl could dream.

"You ready for this, baby?" Tyler questioned.

"So ready." I flashed him an excited smile.

"Okay, lovebirds. Enough of the googly eyes at each other," Chris teased. "Let's get this party started!"

"Hell, yeah!" Tyler exclaimed. "Let's do this."

We all took our seats as Tyler started the engine and eased the boat out of the slip. Once we made it out of the "no wake" zone, he opened up the throttle and sped off across the lake towards Gull Island. I leaned back on the lounger, letting my long hair fly out behind me. I couldn't erase the silly grin from my face. Using my sunglasses to shield my eyes, I took him in.

I knew my man was sexy, but seeing him command the boat like he owned the lake was totally turning me on. He was shirtless, showing off his lean, defined muscles. His board shorts hug low on his hips, accentuating that "V" that I loved so much. He was all mine. Something I still had a hard time grasping at times.

He found a spot in the lake that was somewhat shallow and slowed the engine. There were a lot of boats out on the lake tonight, trying to enjoy the hot summer evening. Tyler and Chris anchored the boat in about four feet of water. Deep enough to enjoy the water, but shallow enough that we could get out and walk around.

We turned up the radio and cracked the cooler. Even though we were all underage, the marine patrol sheriffs wouldn't really bother us, as long as we kept our drinks covered. This area was a haven for underage drinking, and unless you acted stupid, no one would say a word. It was an unsaid rule among boaters, who were all there to have a good time.

Chris and Tyler both grabbed beers, while Tori and I went for the wine coolers. I stripped off my cover-up, baring my black string bikini. I gazed over at Tyler, knowing he would be watching, and it would drive him crazy. I saw his tongue dart out and run over his bottom lip, as he let out a soft groan. Yeah, mission accomplished.

Tori leaned over to me. "You are soooo evil," she whispered. "I like this side of you!"

"Come on, girl," I beckoned. "Let's go catch some rays."

"Right behind you, girlfriend," she answered.

We made our way to the sundeck on the front of the boat, spread out our towels, and soaked in the sun.

# Chapter 26
## Tyler

I watched as Kyla pulled her cover-up over her head, arched her back, and stuck out her tits. I took in every delicious curve of her body, as she peeked over her shoulder at me. Yeah, she knew what she was doing to me. I couldn't pull my eyes from her as I said to Chris, "I swear that girl is trying to kill me."

I set my beer down, threw off my hat, and jumped off the back of the boat into the lake. The cold water was just what I needed to calm my raging hard-on. I dunked my head, grabbed my hat and turned it backward on my head. Chris followed me in as I grabbed my beer off the deck of the boat.

Chris and I clinked our bottles. "Dude, I don't even know who that girl is. I've known Kyla forever and she's always been quiet and shy. Her nose has always been in a book," Chris stated matter-of-factly. "Whatever you've done, looks good on her." He smiled smugly.

I gave Chris a light punch to the shoulder. "Really? What if I said something like that about Tori?"

"Well, that would just be weird." Chris took a long draw off his beer and shook his head.

"But it's okay for you to say it about Kyla? What the fuck?" I questioned.

"I've known her longer." He shrugged. "Seriously, I think you've been really good for her."

"Thanks, man. I can't believe we have less than a month left before I leave for school. It's going to be really hard being away from her," I admitted. "It could be weeks before I see her. That's a loooong time, if you know what I mean."

"Two words for you. Skype sex." Chris waggled his eyebrows.

"Are you kidding me? She'll never agree to that," surprise laced my voice.

"That's what you think now, but Tori said no at first too. Now, she's like a fuckin' addict," Chris groaned. "Not that I'm complaining. I love that girl. She's insatiable," he said knocking back the last of his beer. "I'm gonna grab another, you want one?"

"Sure. I could go for another." *Skype sex?* I guess it could be worth a try. No way it could replace having her underneath me, but it would be better than nothing.

Chris handed me my beer and popped back into the water. "Can you do me a favor?" I asked.

"Sure, man. What do you need?"

"Can you watch out for her while I'm gone? Not just here, but at Western too?" I felt kind of strange asking Chris this, but I trusted him. And with Kyla and Tori being so close, I knew he would be seeing her a lot.

"You afraid she's gonna cheat?" he questioned.

"What? No!" I almost choked on my beer. "We're solid. It's just that, the shit that happened the other day at the marina has me worried. I forget sometimes how tiny she is. I won't be able to be there for her, and it would make me feel better to know that you had her back."

"Tori and I have got it handled. Those two will be roommates, and I'll be in the same dorm. You know I don't mind kicking a little ass if needed," he assured me. "We won't let anything happen to her."

"Thanks, man." I knuckle bumped him. "You're the best."

"Yeah, I am, aren't I?"

Asshole!

The sky turned pink and orange as the sun started setting over the lake. We had made it back to the marina just before the sun dipped below the horizon.

"Thanks for letting us come out with you guys tonight," Chris said as he took Tori's hand to help her off the boat. He looked back at us. "You guys wanna go grab something to eat?"

"Nah," I answered, slipping my arm around Kyla's shoulder. "I think we're hanging out here for a little longer."

Kyla snuggled into my side and wrapped herself around me. "Tyler's going to show me the rest of the boat." She giggled.

"Gotcha." Chris let out a knowing laugh. "Don't do anything we wouldn't do."

"Well, that leaves the possibilities wide open, man," I joked.

"Don't you know it?" Chris clasped my hand, giving it a hard shake.

Tori leaned over to give Kyla a hug. "See ya later girl." Then whispered loudly in Kyla's ear, "Call me!"

Kyla nodded and waved goodbye to our friends.

I looked at Kyla and laughed. "That girl is about as subtle as a hurricane."

I wrapped my arms back around her and pulled her close. I buried my face in her hair, taking in the sweet coconut smell that was all her. "Come on, let me show you the cabin." I led her down the steps that opened up into a small room and bathroom. There was a full-size bed crammed into the small space.

Kyla spun around, threw her arms out and flopped back on the bed. "This is so cool!"

"You like it?" I asked, sitting down next to her and rubbing my hand over her leg.

"I love it! Think we could just spend the night here?" She looked at me seductively.

102

A deep growl escaped my chest. "I'd love to, but I think your dad might kill me."

"You're right." She let out a big huff. "He's been really cool lately. No sense in rocking the boat."

"Oh baby, we're still going to rock the boat." I laid over her and pressed my lips to hers. I started to slip her cover-up over her head and ran my hands along her stomach. "You know what this bikini does to me?"

She let out a little giggle and feigned innocence. "What? This old thing? It's just a bathing suit, Ty."

"You little minx. You know exactly what this does to me." I ran my fingers under the strings that covered her hips.

She batted her eyelashes at me and smiled. "I have no idea what you're talking about."

"Then let me show you." I crawled over her body and pulled the strings that held her suit together. I ran my hands over every surface and curve of her beautiful body as she moaned softly. I pushed my trunks down, slipped a condom on, and eased her legs apart. I slid into her heat as her legs wrapped around my waist. I made slow, lazy love to her. We rocked the boat and let the waves of pleasure consume us long into the night.

# Chapter 27
## Kyla

July was coming to an end. Tyler and I made the most of every single moment we'd had together. We'd fucked and made love—yes, there was a difference—more times than I could count.

I loved when he was rough with me, because I felt alive and safe in his arms. I knew he would never hurt me and if I said "stop", he would.

I never did.

I loved when he was soft and tender with me too. When he whispered kisses across my skin, making tingles run along my spine. When he made me feel like I was beautiful.

I wasn't.

But he thought I was. And that was all that mattered. For now.

I wasn't stupid. I knew when he left for MSU next week, our lives would change. He'd be a quarterback at a Big 10 school. The girls would fall in love with him. He'd be sought after and hunted down by the girls that wanted to be able to say they'd slept with the quarterback. I knew he loved me, but I hoped he could resist the temptations that would surround him.

I hoped he loved me enough.

If we weren't going to different schools, I wouldn't have been so worried. Everyone would know we were together. But with me being at Western, they wouldn't. I had decided not to try out for Western's cheerleading team. I needed to be at Tyler's games. Those girls needed to see us together. To know Tyler and I were a couple.

I trusted him. I did. It was the slutty chicks I didn't trust. They wouldn't care if he was mine. They'd try to take him anyway.

I would never have asked him to give up his dreams for me. Those were his to keep, not mine to take. I should have just gone to MSU with him. With my grades, I could have gotten a scholarship to go there too. But WMU had the graphic design and advertising program I wanted.

I thought that this would be easy. The two universities were only an hour and a half apart. But the distance that would be between us was becoming a reality and I was scared.

I wasn't worried about being tempted by other guys. I knew from that first kiss in his car on Homecoming night. I knew he was it for me. I knew he would steal my heart and hold it in the palm of his hand. I knew that he was my forever.

I hoped I was his.

I finished packing my bags for our trip to the lake house. Tyler would be here shortly to pick me up. Then we would go to Chris's house to meet him and Tori. I lugged my bags down the stairs and placed them in the front hall. We would be gone for six days. Two days later he would be gone. I was going to squeeze every ounce of pleasure I could from the next week.

I heard his car pull up and the door close. When he opened our front door, I threw my arms around his neck and kissed him deeply. He returned the kiss but looked around to see where my parents were. "They're in the kitchen," I whispered. He nodded and kissed me deeper.

We broke apart and walked to the kitchen to say goodbye. It was still fairly early, and my mom and dad were just finishing their morning coffee. "Okay, we're ready to leave," I said cheerily.

My dad motioned to the two empty chairs at the table. "Have a seat. I want to talk to the two of you."

*Oh shit!*

We had no choice, so we quietly sat down and gave each other the *What the Fuck?* look. We knew what was coming... the "Talk".

My dad looked at both of us and started, "You know I have my reservations about this trip, but you're both adults now and can make your own decisions." He looked at Tyler and continued, "You've earned my respect this summer, Tyler. But this is still my little girl."

Tyler kept his eyes trained on my dad and showed confidence with his words, "I understand, Mr. O'Malley. I hope you know I would never hurt Kyla or disrespect her. I think you know I love her."

My dad nodded. "I do. And she loves you," he said. "I also know we," he turned to my mom lovingly and took her hand, "we were eighteen when Kyla was born. We were young once and I understand, but it wasn't planned and it wasn't easy. All I'm saying is... be careful. You both have bright futures and babies change everything."

"Dad, we know all this." I swallowed down the bile in my throat as I said the next part. "We're careful." *Ugh! I just admitted to my parents that we were having sex! Please! Can we just leave now!*

My mom stood from the table and looked at my dad. "I think they got the message, and they have a long drive. We should let them get going." *Thank you, mom!!!*

I kissed my mom and dad goodbye. Tyler shook my dad's hand and hugged my mother. We gathered all my bags and headed out to the car, as my parents stood in the driveway and watched us pack up. "What do you have in here? You do realize we're only going to be gone six days, right?" he said as he threw my bags in the trunk with his one duffle bag.

"A girl's got to be prepared, right?" I gave him my best flirty smile and fluttered my eyelashes at him. I shrugged my shoulders at him. "Girls have a lot of stuff."

He finally cracked a smile. "This I know," he said and tapped the tip of my nose.

We hopped in the car and slowly pulled out of the driveway, making our way to Chris's house. When we were a safe distance from the house, Tyler finally cracked. "That was intense. Your dad scares me a little bit."

"You handled it like a pro," I assured him. "I'm the one who had to admit to my parents that we're having sex," I groaned.

"Kyla, they already knew."

"Yeah, but they kind of made me say it. No girl wants to tell her dad she's having sex. It's just awkward." I made a face and shivered. "It's just kind of…gross. You know?"

Tyler reached his hand across the console and grabbed my knee. "Oh, so having sex with me is gross, huh?"

"Oh, totally!" I teased him back. "Lucky for you, I'm really into gross."

He laughed hard and glanced over at me. "Okay. Now you're giving me complex."

I leaned over and kissed his cheek. "You know I love you. And I really love having sex with you. And… I'm really looking forward to this week, so I can have my wicked way with you." I laughed. "No interruptions. No late-night curfews. Just us, snuggled together under the sheets."

He turned his head and caught me with a quick kiss. "Me too."

# Chapter 28
## Tyler

We pulled up at Chris's a few minutes later. I popped the trunk and checked the side pocket of my duffle. The small box was still there. I had to double check.

Once everyone was loaded up, Chris and Tori pulled out in his pickup behind us. We headed toward I-75. We had about a four-hour drive north to Traverse City, where we would stop and get groceries, then another half hour to the house on Lake Michigan.

Once we got on the expressway, Kyla turned up the radio, leaned back in her seat, and put her pretty painted feet on the dashboard. She wiggled her toes in time with the music. It was cute as fuck. Her legs were so short, she could stretch them out completely.

"You know I hate that, don't you?" I lied.

"What?" she questioned.

I motioned to her legs. I loved teasing her. "Your feet on the dashboard. Where's the respect?"

"Really? I don't have my shoes on." She pulled her legs back, a worried look on her face.

"No. Not really," I admitted. "It's actually really cute. You have sexy feet. And sexy legs." I reached my hand over and rubbed up and down her thigh.

She breathed a sigh of relief, put her feet back up on the dashboard, leaned back and closed her eyes. We drove in silence, not needing to fill the space with words. We were just content together in each other's company. I could tell when she fell asleep, because her toes stopped tapping and her head lolled to the side. I loved watching her sleep. She was so beautiful.

I didn't tell Kyla, but my dad had had the sex talk with me the night before. He was a little more forward about it.

*I was sitting in my room and had just put a large box of condoms in my duffle bag, when my dad walked in. I tried to zip the bag quickly, but I knew he had seen.*

*"I already know you and Kyla are having sex," he said. "You don't have to hide that shit from me."*

*I huffed out a breath. "Yeah, we are."*

*He sat down on the bed next to me. "You're eighteen and the two of you have been together a while now. How long? How long have you two been active?" he questioned.*

*"About two months."*

*My dad rubbed his hand over his chin. "Huh. I thought it had been longer than that. Were you her first?"*

*I grabbed at the back of my neck. This conversation was awkward. "Yeah. And she was mine."*

*He raised his eyebrows. "Really?"*

*I nodded my head. "I love her, dad."*

*"I trust you, but you two are going to be alone all week. Keep your head. You've set yourself some pretty big goals. Babies can change things. I don't want to see everything you've worked for to go down the drain. I don't know what her plans are, but I'm sure they don't include a baby."*

*"We're careful. Neither one of us wants kids right now. Trust me."*

*"What happens when you go away to school? There's going to be lots of girls there. Some of them would like nothing more than to get pregnant if you end up making a name for yourself."*

*I was taken aback. "I'm not going to cheat on Kyla."*

*"I didn't say you would, but temptation will be there."*

*"Unless she's a cute little blond with green eyes, I'm not interested."*

*"Just be careful. That's all I'm saying." He stood and walked towards the door, then stopped to face me again. "By the*

*way, I like her. She seems to make you happy. It's your job to keep her safe. Treat her right."* Then he walked away.

*"I will,"* I said to myself. *Always.*

I drove with the radio turned low, lost in my own thoughts. I wanted to make this week special for her. I knew she was worried about us being apart. Although she would never tell me, I knew she wished I wasn't leaving. She was good at hiding her true feelings, but I could see right through her. I could see her insecurities. I would try to take them all away this week. I would assure her that we would be okay. We had to be. Anything else was not an option, because she was my *forever*.

When we got closer to Traverse City, I gently shook her leg. "Time to wake up, Sleeping Beauty."

Her eyes fluttered open as she stretched her arms up over her head, pushing her tits out. "Oh, my god. What time is it?" she said trying to acclimate herself.

"It's almost one."

"I didn't mean to fall asleep. Why didn't you wake me up?" she questioned.

"I like watching you sleep. Besides, you're going to need all your energy for later." I waggled my eyebrows at her.

She flipped down the mirror, rubbing underneath her eyes to fix her smudged makeup. "Is that so?"

"Yep. The only sleep we're getting will be while lying on the beach," I promised.

She rested her head on my shoulder and sighed. "I can't wait."

After stopping to get groceries, we drove the final stretch to the beach house. We pulled in the driveway, and you could see the lake just past the house. It was a great house, with a wraparound porch in front and a massive deck in the back that led right out to the water.

We unpacked the groceries and carried them inside. "Tori, I've really missed this place!" Kyla exclaimed as she unloaded the bags onto the kitchen counter. She turned to me.

"Tori's family used to bring me here every summer, since we were like sisters and inseparable."

Tori threw her arm around Kyla's shoulders and pulled her into a side hug. "I swear we were attached at the hip when we were kids."

Chris snuck up behind Tori and grabbed her around the waist. "This week those hips are going to be attached to mine and my dick is going to attached to your..." Tori quickly threw her hand up over his mouth. We all broke out into laughter.

"You're so crass, man," I said shaking my head at him.

Tori and Kyla finished putting everything away in the kitchen, while Chris and I brought in everything else from the car. Tori and Chris took her room. Kyla and I took the guest room. I carried everything in and set it on the bed. I went over to the sliding glass door, pushed it open, and stepped out onto the balcony.

Kyla came up behind me and wrapped her arms around my waist, leaning her head against my back. "It's beautiful, isn't it?" The lake stretched out for miles in front of us, the water blue and sparkling. "If you look over there," she said pointing to the right, "you can see the Sleeping Bear Dunes. And if you look straight out into the water, you can just see her cubs, The Manitou Islands."

I knew the legend. We had all learned it in school during Michigan history, but seeing it was different than reading about it.

I reached back and brought her around to my front and wrapped my arms around her small shoulders, tucking her under my chin. I could stay like this forever, feeling her warmth as she snuggled into my chest. "I wanna be inside you," I whispered as I buried my face in her hair.

She looked up at me with those brilliant green eyes. "Then make love to me."

I captured her lips with mine and carried her to the bed. We pushed our bags to the floor and started to undress each

111

other. The cool breeze from the lake swept across our naked bodies. I pulled a condom from my bag and gently pushed her back against the mattress. She opened her legs for me and I slowly slid in. Her blond hair cascaded across the pillow. She was all mine. I hovered above her and she wrapped her legs around me. There was nothing more perfect than this right here. I started to move, slowly rocking in and out of her. She pushed her hips up into mine, looking for the friction she needed. I kissed her lips and down her neck, as I continued to slide in and out. She leaned her head back and moaned, "Oh my god, baby. That's so good. I'm so close."

I picked up the pace and pushed into her hard, burying myself to the hilt. I ground into her, trying to give her what she needed. She began pulsing around me, clenching down on me, and we both lost it. I rode her through her orgasm as I chased mine with one final thrust. I collapsed and rolled on my back next to her. I threaded my fingers with hers. "I love you, Kyla."

She looked deep in my eyes. "I love you, too. You're my everything."

Just as I leaned into kiss her, a loud knock scared the crap out of us.

"Stop fucking! We're going down to the beach," Chris yelled through the door.

I rolled my eyes. "Yeah! We're coming!"

"I don't need to know that shit. Just get your suits on and meet us on the deck."

Kyla giggled. "I guess we better get dressed."

# Chapter 29
## Kyla

It was late afternoon before we made it to the beach. And although I wanted nothing more than to spend time walking along the shoreline, my stomach had other ideas. "I'm hungry and you guys must be starving. How about I go back up to the house and get dinner started?"

Tori piped in, "I'll come with you. How about just burgers tonight, since I don't have the energy for much more?"

"Sounds good to me. Want us to come up and start the grill?" Tyler said.

"That would be perfect," I said.

We all made our way back up to house. Tori and I got started on making the hamburger patties and a salad, while the guys got the grill ready.

Tori pulled out the lettuce and cucumber from the fridge. "So, you guys were already at it, huh?" She had a smug look on her face as she started to slice the cucumber.

"Hey, don't judge. This is our last week to really get some alone time together," I said pointing a knife at her.

Tori held her hands up in surrender. "I'm not judging. Just making an observation."

"Well don't. I promise to pretend I don't hear you and Chris, if you pretend not to hear us. Deal?" I continued to cut the lettuce and put it in a bowl.

"Deal." Tori giggled. "But seriously, what's going to happen after this week?"

I looked out to the deck to make sure the guys we're still occupied. Then I turned to Tori and whispered, "I plan on fucking him so many times that he won't even be able to think of anyone else when he goes to school. I'm up for anything creative. Any advice?"

"Oh girl, you've come to the right place." She started ticking off her ideas on her fingers, "Shower sex, reverse cowgirl, doggie style…oh and don't forget sex on the beach. It's more than just a drink you know."

I started giggling. "You are so bad! Speaking of drinks, was Chris's brother able to hook us up?"

"Of course. Would I leave you hanging like that?"

"Well, let's break them out. I could go for something right about now."

Tori reached up into the cabinet above the refrigerator and started pulling out bottles. "Pick your poison- Absolute, Captain Morgan's, plus there are beer and wine coolers in the drawer of the fridge."

"I'm gonna have a Captain and diet. Can you grab a beer for Tyler?"

"Sure thing, girlie." Tori reached in and pulled out two bottles.

"Thanks." I grabbed the drinks and the platter of hamburger patties and headed out toward the deck.

After dinner and a few more drinks, we decided to head down to the beach and make a bonfire. The four of us sat around the fire, listened to music, and rehashed some of the best moments from the last year. As the sun began to set over the lake, I snuggled up between Tyler's legs, while he held me tight. I rested my head back on his shoulder and sighed. "I love it here with you. I wish this could last forever."

"Me too, Ky. We have the next five days together. Let's make them count." He leaned his head into mine and kissed me.

114

"I think we're going to head back to the house. See you guys in a bit?" Tori asked.

"Sure thing. Just remember our deal, okay?" I gave her a knowing look.

"Wouldn't forget, girlfriend." She waved over her shoulder and made the trek back up the beach with Chris.

Tyler looked at me in confusion. "What deal would that be?"

"Oh nothing. Just girl talk." I feigned innocence.

"Girl talk, huh?"

"Yep." I said definitively. I turned in his arms, sitting between his legs, and threw my arms around his neck. I pressed my lips to his and bit gently at his bottom lip. He reached up and turned his hat backwards, devouring my mouth with his. The sun dipped below the horizon, leaving us with only the light from the fire. I gently pushed him back on the sand and laid on his chest. Our kisses became more desperate. He reached his hand up under my shirt and palmed my breast. I moaned, as I ran my hands over his hard chest. "You wanna move this inside?"

"Yeah, but we are having sex on this beach before we go home," he groaned.

"Definitely, but not tonight. I have other plans for you." I grabbed his hand and pulled him to his feet. We kicked sand over the fire, and I led him back to the house. Dragging him behind me, I made my way to our bedroom, which just happened to have an en suite bathroom. After shutting the door, I made sure it was locked. I walked toward the bathroom, stripping my shirt off along the way. "Shower with me?"

Tyler's eyes went wide. "Yes. Please."

I wiggled my finger at him, motioning for him to follow. "You said this was on your to-do list, so figured we might as well." I turned the water on and slid my shorts off. I stood there and let him take me in before I reached for the hem of his shirt. I slid it up his chest and over his head, then went to work on his shorts. His hands were all over me, caressing every curve of my body.

I stepped in, pulling him with me. We let the water wash over our bodies, as we melted into each other. I ran my hands down his chest, past his sexy "V" and down to his hardness. I gripped it firmly in my hand and started to stroke him up and down.

"God, baby, that feels incredible," he growled.

I sank to my knees. I licked the precum from his head and wrapped my lips around his length. I sank down on him deep and felt him against the back of my throat. I wrapped my tongue around his hardness, and swirled it up under his tip, caressing the soft skin. Then sank back down again. I continued bobbing my head up and down, stroking him with my hand. I looked up at him, from under my lashes and saw the ecstasy on his face. It encouraged me to suck harder and deeper, taking him to the back of my throat over and over again.

"You gotta stop, Ky. I'm gonna come," he groaned out, trying to pull me to my feet.

I pushed his hands away and continued my assault. Going deeper and faster, stroking him harder and tighter. I felt him tense up, twitch, and then hot streams ran down my throat. I swallowed and stroked him through his orgasm, taking in every last drop.

I stood and faced him. "Good?"

"Fucking awesome, baby. But you didn't have to... "

I put a finger to his lips. "I want to make you feel good. I don't want you to forget about me when you're gone."

"Not gonna happen. Ever." He rubbed his hands over my shoulders, down my back, and cupped my ass, pulling me closer. He quickly turned me, pushed me against the wall and ran his hands down my back. His hands lingered at the small of my back as I arched into his touch.

I braced my hands against the wall and looked at him over my shoulder. He was ready and waiting. "Again? Already?"

"Kyla, this is only the beginning. I could go all night with you. Remember, no sleep except on the beach?"

"I remember," I said breathlessly. I pushed my hips back and spread my legs. He grabbed my hips and slid into my slick heat. No condom. No barriers. The skin on skin sensation was amazing. He held my hips tight, bruising the delicate skin, pulling himself into me harder and harder. "Oh, my... that's so fucking good. Harder, baby!" Pain melted into pleasure, as he picked up the pace and slammed into me over and over again, pushing my breasts against the wall. And then the fullness was gone. I felt him come against my back, as it dripped down my ass. His hands went to the wall above my head. He leaned over me panting and out of breath.

"I'm so sorry. I shouldn't have done that. I got carried away." He hung his head in regret and looked down at me.

"It was amazing. I loved feeling you—and just you—inside me," I assured him.

"It was amazing." He closed his eyes. "But we can't be irresponsible. I need to think with the right head."

I turned and took him in my arms. "You didn't decide that on your own. I could have stopped you. I didn't. And I don't regret it."

"I know, but from here on out—we don't do that shit."

I threw some shorts and a tank top on and started to crawl under the covers. Tyler came out of the bathroom with a towel wrapped low on his hips. He looked at me and let out a low laugh. "What are you doing?"

"Ummm... getting ready for bed?" I asked, confused at his question. I mean, wasn't it obvious?

He motioned to my shorts and tank. "What are you wearing?"

I looked down at my clothes, trying to figure out what the problems was. "Pajamas?"

"You are so fucking cute, you know that?" He stalked over to the bed and reached for the hem of my tank. He pulled it over my head, freeing my breasts from the material. I looked at him with wide eyes. "This is a 'no pajamas' week, woman. Number one—I want to feel your soft skin against mine at night." He slid his fingers into the waistband of my shorts. I lifted my hips, so he could slide those off too. "Number two—they're just a waste of time, since I plan on taking them off anyway."

I gave him a flirty smile. "So that's it, huh? I don't get a say? What are you? The pajama police?"

"Something like that." He pulled the towel at his waist and let it fall to the ground. He crawled up on the bed and straddled me. He grabbed me by the hips and pulled me down, so I was flat on my back. He took my wrists and locked them together on the pillow over my head. He leaned over the top of me, pinning me with his gaze. "Did you want me to handcuff you? Because that can be arranged." His voice was low and seductive. His eyes dark and piercing.

I looked up at him with innocence. I thought about his proposition, then said softly, "I…I don't think I'm ready for that yet." The way he looked at me, put me in a trance. All conscious thought left my mind, as images of being handcuffed floated through my mind. It wasn't altogether that unappealing. What if that was what he wanted? Something I wasn't ready for. Yet. We had never really talked about *that*. I swallowed down the lump in my throat.

"Relax. I'm messing with you." He flashed me that panty dropping smile.

I let out a breath of relief. "You scared me a little bit," I whispered.

He ran his knuckles softly down the side of my face. "Baby, you know I would never do anything to you that we both didn't agree on? Right?"

I turned my head to the side, swallowing down another lump. Tears that I was trying to hide, filled my eyes. I blinked them away. He let go of my wrists and turned my chin to look at him. A single tear ran down the side of my face to the pillow.

Concern filled his eyes. "Kyla, I really was just messing with you." He placed a gentle kiss on my lips.

"I know." I took a deep breath, letting my insecurities show. "I just... I just want to be enough for you." My voice quivered, as I fought to keep it under control.

"Baby, look at me." I looked into his eyes. Eyes so blue, they put the ocean to shame. "You are more than enough for me. You're smart. You're beautiful. You're sexy. You bring out the best in me. You're my everything, my forever."

He got up from the bed and went to his duffle bag. He unzipped it and then came back to sit next to me. "I was going to wait until later in the week for this, but I think now is the perfect time."

I sat up in bed, grasping the sheet to my chest to cover me. He pulled a small box from behind his back. I gasped and threw my hands up over my mouth, letting the sheet fall to my waist. *Oh my god!*

"It's not what you think." He smiled at me. "I have thought about us and our future together. One day, I will marry you. Nothing would make me happier. But for now, this is all I can offer." He opened the box. Nestled inside the velvet lining was a silver ring with an amethyst stone cut in the shape of a heart. The color such a deep shade of purple, it almost looked black. He took the ring out of the box and placed it on the ring finger of my right hand. "I'm giving you my heart. When you look at it, I want you to remember this is my promise to you. I know it will be hard when we go away to school, but I'll always be with you.

I was struck speechless. I had so much I wanted to say, but none of it would come out. I just stared at the beautiful heart shaped ring on my finger. Tears filled my eyes for a whole new reason and slipped down my cheek.

Tyler took my hands in his. "I hope those are happy tears."

I nodded my head frantically. "Yes! I…I just don't know what to say."

"Say you'll have faith in me. In us." He brought my hands to his lips and kissed them. "I know this is scary— being apart— but we can do this. I'm not going anywhere. My heart is staying with you."

"I will… I mean… I do. I… I don't even know how to tell you how much I love you," I said wiping the tears away.

"You show me every day. I couldn't ask for more." He pulled me in and wrapped his arms around me. "When I asked you to Homecoming, I never knew you would completely capture my heart."

I pulled back. "I want you to know, I've always trusted you. It's those skanky bitches I don't trust," I said twisting my mouth sideways.

He chuckled, whether at my words or my expression, I wasn't not sure. "Don't you worry about those skanky bitches. I'll make sure they know we're together. You'll try to be at my games, right?"

"Of course! I gotta cheer my man on."

He took my face in his hands. "We're going to be all right."

"I know," I said placing my hands over his.

"Good. Now that we've settled that, I think we have some unfinished business. I owe you some lovin'. And I always pay my debts."

He reached down and grabbed me by the ankles, pulling me flat to the mattress again. I giggled at the rush as my head hit the pillow. He pushed my feet apart and settled between my legs.

"See? Clothes are such a waste of time." He buried his head between my thighs and paid his debt many times over.

# Chapter 30
## Tyler

*Thunk! Thunk! Thunk!*

My eyes popped open at the sound. Kyla was wrapped in my arms, her head on my chest. She was beautiful when she slept.

The morning light was just starting to peek through the blinds. It was still early. Really early. I reached over and grabbed my phone to check the time.

*Thunk! Thunk! Thunk!*

Kyla stirred on my chest. Her eyes barely opened as she looked up at me. "What time is it?" she asked in her groggy morning voice.

*Thunk! Thunk! Thunk!*

"Early." We both looked at the wall behind the bed. "Too early for this shit."

Kyla smiled smugly, resting her head back on my chest. "You can't say anything. That was the deal."

"What deal?"

*Thunk! Thunk! Thunk!*

"I promised we'd pretend not to hear them, if they pretended not to hear us," she explained. *Thunk! Thunk! Thunk! Thunk!*

"Fuck that! It's like 5:30 in the morning." I reached my arm up over my head and pounded my fist against the wall. "People are trying to sleep over here!" I shouted.

"Sorry!" The muffled response came through the wall.

I snuggled Kyla back in my arms, wrapping her in my warmth. I kissed the top of her head and drifted back to sleep.

I woke a few hours later to an empty bed. I didn't like it. I wanted to wake with her still in my arms. I quickly threw some shorts on and headed to the kitchen. The smell of coffee filled the air.

Tori and Chris were sitting at the table getting their morning caffeine. "Morning, cock blocker," Chris chided. I flipped him the bird then grabbed a mug from the cabinet and filled it.

"Boy, someone's crabby this morning." Tori smirked over her cup of coffee.

I added cream and sugar. "Someone got woke up at the ass crack of dawn by his friends fucking against the wall," I replied curtly.

"Technically, that was the bed, not us," Chris corrected.

"Whatever, man. It was early." I looked around the room looking for her. "Where's Kyla?"

Tori pointed towards the slider. "She's sitting out on the back deck. Been out there a while."

I nodded my thanks and walked towards the deck. I could see her through the window, sitting at the table, feet up on the chair, knees tucked to her chest, as she looked out over the lake with a mug in her hands. Her hair was in a messy knot on top of her head. She was gorgeous with the sun shining on her face, free of makeup and natural.

I slid the door open. "Where'd you go?"

She turned to look at me and smiled. "I didn't want to wake you."

I went over and sank in the chair next to her. "Whatcha doing out here by yourself?"

She looked back out over the lake. "I just love it here. It's so peaceful in the morning. I like listening to the waves, it's soothing. It calms me. Helps me put life into perspective." She turned and faced me. "Thank you for last night. I needed that. But you always know what I need." She looked down at the ring on her finger. "Thank you for always being there for me. And for being here with me now."

"Baby, there's no place I'd rather be. You okay?"

"I'm perfect," she assured me. "So, what do you want to do today?

"Well," I said running my hand over my stubble, "what do you think about jet skiing? Do you know if there's a place around here to rent them?"

"Ooooh! That sounds like fun." Her eyes lit up. "I think there's a place just down the road. I'll have to ask Tori." Kyla got up and walked to the slider, then quickly turned back around. "Are you hungry? I'll make you breakfast."

"How about we make it together?"

She gave me a sweet smile. "Come on," she motioned with her head.

After a breakfast of eggs, bacon, and toast, we all got changed and took Chris's truck down to the jet ski rental. We rented two. One for Chris and Tori and one for us. After I got Kyla situated in her life jacket, we headed toward the dock. "Have you ever done this before?" I asked.

"No." She shook her head. "Have you?"

"Once. But it was back in Bay City on an inland lake. You scared?"

"Not with you." I loved that she put all her faith in me. She felt safe with me.

I lower myself onto the jet ski, then held my hand out for her to step on behind me. "Hold on tight. And don't let go."

She wrapped her hands around my waist and gripped my legs with her thighs. Fuck, that felt good. "You ready?"

"Yes," she answered as the jet ski bobbed in the waves under us.

I started the engine, and she laid her head against my back. I started out into the open water. I took it slow, riding the waves that were close to the shore. When we got out a distance, I yelled back over my shoulder, "Hang on, baby!"

I opened the throttle and soared out across the lake. I loved the feeling of the wind in my face and the freedom of the open water. A speed boat passed us, creating huge waves in its wake. We took the first wave and soared into the air, landing hard back in the water, then skimmed over the smaller waves. I slowed and looked over my shoulder. "You okay?"

Kyla had a giant smile plastered across her face. She nodded and laughed. "This is awesome!" The waves rocked us back and forth.

I opened it up again and took off across the lake. We drove down by the Sleeping Bear Dunes and then headed back. Kyla gripped me tighter, never loosening her hold. She laughed and screamed with delight. It was music to my ears to hear her enjoying this. I slowed us down to a stop and turned to give her a kiss. Just her and me out in the lake as we bobbed up and down. "You really like this, don't you?"

"I love it! Can I drive?"

I looked at her skeptically. "You sure?"

"Yeah! I wanna do it." She was glowing. How could I say no to that?

We switched places as I put the key ring around her wrist. I held on to her tiny waist. "Be careful, baby. You gotta hold on tight…" Before I even finished my sentence, she had us roaring across the lake. Another speedboat came by and she took the wake like a pro. I was actually pretty impressed.

I saw her go to make the turn and everything happened in slow motion. She turned the handles tight to the left, taking the curve way too sharp. The momentum from the speed, didn't allow us to follow the turn she was taking. I tried to hold on to her, but my hands slipped from her waist and I was thrown off into the cold, deep water. I went under and was disoriented by the waves, water rushing over my head. When I finally surfaced, I looked around and saw the jet ski bobbing in the water about fifteen feet away. Kyla wasn't on it. I fucking panicked and searched around in the water.

When I turned to the right, there she was, full on laughing, as she treaded water. "You okay?" I yelled to her. I couldn't keep the worry out of my voice.

"Oh my god! That was awesome!" she cried out.

I swam out to her and grabbed her hand, pulling her back to me. "You scared the shit out of me!" I wrapped my arms around her and hugged her tight.

She pulled back. "I'm fine." A smile lit up her face.

She pulled my hand, and we swam back to the jet ski. I climbed up first, then held out my hand to help her up. She climbed on behind me and handed me the key. I was pissed, now that I knew she was fine. The feeling I had when I thought something might have happened to her, settled low in my gut. We drove back to the shore in silence. We docked and took off our life jackets. I knew she could sense my level of pisstivity. I started to walk away, leaving her standing there.

"Hey! I'm sorry!" she said. "I just got carried away. The adrenaline rush. The wind in my hair. The open water. I was just having fun!"

I strode back to her, my anger simmering over and leaned down close to her face. "You scared the fuck out of me! That was reckless! When I didn't see you, I panicked." I pointed at my chest. "It's MY job to keep you safe!"

She turned her back on me, crossing her arms over her chest, and her shoulders started to shake. I reached out to touch her shoulder and she shrugged it off, pulling away.

My anger hadn't dissipated, but I knew I had just hurt her. *Fuck!* "Kyla?" I said gruffly.

She turned and faced me, tears in her eyes, but never falling. "What?" she snapped. "You think it's okay to yell at me like that? I'm not a child!" Her voice was cold and hard. She

126

had never used that tone with me before. "I made a mistake. Get the fuck over it! I'm fine! You're fine!" She let out a frustrated sigh. "This was supposed to be fun. Mission NOT accomplished!" She stomped off toward Chris's truck, threw down the tailgate, and hopped up.

I turned in the key to the rental office. I felt like shit. *Why did I yell at her like that?* Because she scared me, that's why. But she really didn't deserve it. I knew that. I walked over to the truck, grabbed my hat out of the cab, and then hopped on the tailgate next to her.

I put my arm around her and buried my head in her hair. "I'm sorry."

"Me, too. But you can't yell at me like that" her voice was distant.

"I know you didn't mean for that to happen. I just got scared. I didn't mean to yell at you," I whispered.

"Me neither," she said softly.

"Did we just have our first fight?"

She looked up at me with those sad green eyes. "I think so."

"You've never talked to me like that before. I honestly didn't know you had it in you."

"You've never pissed me off before," she said honestly. "I'm sorry I scared you."

I took her face in my hands. "I don't want to fight with you."

"I don't want to fight with you either."

"I hear make up sex is pretty great," I smirked at her. "Maybe we can try it out."

When we got back to the house, Kyla and I snuck off to our room. She sat on the bed, wringing her hands in her lap. "Tyler, I really am sorry about what happened today. The last thing I wanted to do here, was fight with you. Especially since this our last week together for a while."

I sat next to her, taking her hand. "Maybe it was a good thing. I mean, better here to have our first fight than when we're miles apart. At least we know we can handle it and come out of it okay."

"We're okay?" she questioned.

"Yeah, we're okay. It's going to take more than that to break us."

She nodded. "It gave me a sick feeling in my stomach. I don't like fighting with you."

"Me neither, baby. I love you. No more fighting." I pulled her onto my lap and wrapped my arms around her waist. She put her arms around my shoulders and pressed her lips to mine.

Suddenly, the kiss became frantic, as our tongues tangled. Kyla pushed her soft hands up under my shirt and rubbed my muscular chest. I reached back and pulled the shirt over my head. She reached for the hem over her own shirt, lifting it away. I worked the ties on her bikini top and let if fall to her lap, freeing her tits.

Our remaining clothes disappeared fast, as we desperately groped each other. I needed in her. Now! She straddled my chest and I stuck my fingers in her wet, warm pussy. "I love how you're always so ready for me," I growled. I grabbed her hips and pulled her to my face. I had never done that to her before.

"Ty?" she stiffened. Then gasped as I stuck my tongue inside her, and her body relaxed from the pleasure I was giving her. Her head dropped back, as she grabbed at the headboard of the bed, "Oh my god!" Her breath came in quick short bursts as I worked her relentlessly, finding that perfect spot. I felt her pussy clench around my tongue, as she came on my face.

She moved back down my chest and I quickly grabbed a condom. Kyla hovered over my dick. I grabbed it in my hand and guided it into her wetness. With her hands braced on my chest, she slid down on my cock. She let out a loud moan as her eyes rolled back in ecstasy. She worked me up and down at a furious pace. Her tits bouncing. I reached up and took them in my hands, squeezing and rolling her nipples between my fingers.

She pushed her pussy down on me, gyrating her hips. I seized the moment, grabbed her by the waist and flipped her over onto her back. She let out a loud gasp as she landed hard onto the mattress. She spread her legs wide, knees bent, and feet flat on the bed. She pushed her hips up meeting me thrust for thrust. I pounded my dick into her fast and furious. I pushed her knees to her chest, allowing me to get deeper. With my hands on the back of her thighs, I watched as I slid into her over and over again. The sight of me disappearing into her, was erotic as fuck. Her hand went between us. She desperately rubbed small circles against her clit, seeking her own release again.

Her head flew back, and she let out a scream, as she came hard around my dick. I swallowed her scream with my lips. Her pussy clenched me in wave after wave. I was so close. I pushed her legs harder to her chest and thrust just three more times. I exploded inside of her. Not once but twice. I released everything I had into her sweet pussy.

Exhausted, I released her legs and collapsed on top of her. Sweat dripped down my face and I couldn't catch my breath. Kyla wrapped her arms around me holding me tight to her. I flipped on my back, taking her with me. She rested her head on my chest as I stroked her hair. We were both breathing hard, trying to come down from the high we were just on. This right here, with Kyla, was perfection.

# Chapter 31
## Kyla

*Oh my god!* The sex kept getting better and better. Maybe it was knowing that we could take our time. Maybe it was because we knew there would be no interruptions. Maybe it was because we weren't afraid of getting caught. Whatever it was… it was incredible. Primal. Animalistic. We didn't think, we just felt. We gave and we took, pleasing each other so thoroughly. It was everything I never knew it could be.

Our week together was speeding by so fast, I wished I could slow time and make this last longer. We fell asleep every night from sheer exhaustion and woke every morning wrapped in each other's arms. I was really going to miss this. Four days was all we had left, and then he would be gone. I didn't know how I was going to go back to sleeping by myself, without his warm body wrapped around me.

This was our last full day at the lake house, we would go home tomorrow. Tyler would have one more day to pack everything for college and he would leave the next morning. I guess it wasn't even four days, more like three.

Ty and I got up early and went running on the beach. We only made it about two miles before my legs gave out on me. Running on the sand was so much harder than it looked. My muscles burned and my heart raced. I stopped and put my hands on my knees as I tried to catch my breath. I looked up and saw Tyler jogging back to me.

"You okay, Ky?"

I put up my finger, motioning for him to wait just a minute. When I got my breathing under control, I stood up and shook my legs out. "Sorry. I can't go any farther. My legs were starting to cramp."

"That's fine. Running on this sand is a bitch. Let's walk it out for a little bit." Tyler took my hand and we walked down the beach a little farther.

We came to a big grouping of rocks that jutted out into the lake. I started climbing up the rocks, crawled out to the furthest one, and sat on the edge. Ty climbed up next to me and put his arm around my shoulders. We looked out over the water listening to the waves crashing into the shore.

"What are you thinking about?" he asked.

"Next year," I answered as I absentmindedly ran my finger up and down the scar on my knee.

"Which part?" he prodded.

"All of it."

"When are your tryouts for cheerleading?"

I stared out at the water. "I already missed them. They were last month."

Tyler dropped his arm from my shoulder. He looked at me with confusion. "What? Why would you do that?"

"I had to make a choice. I wouldn't be able to come to your games if I was on Western's cheerleading team."

Ty rubbed his hand over his face. "Ky?"

"It was a trade-off. I don't regret it." I continued staring out at the lake.

"But you love cheering and you're really good at it."

"I am good at it and I do love it." I turned to face him. "But I love you more. I need to be there for you. With you."

He crushed me to his chest and kissed the top of my head. "What am I going to do with you?"

"Just love me," I replied.

"I already do. More and more every day."

I was determined to capture as many memories as possible on our last full day at the beach. I gathered our towels, water, sunscreen, and assorted other items and put them on the bed. Tyler watched me as I stuffed everything into my oversized beach bag. He had an amused look on his face. "You know we're only going to be about fifty yards from the house, right?"

"I know, but I don't want to keep running back up here. What else do we need? Oh, I almost forgot." I scrounged around in my suitcase for the camera I'd brought. I pulled it out and held it up for him to see, then stuffed it in the bag too.

He scrunched up his eyebrows. "What's that for? I've got my phone, babe."

"Yeah, I know, but my camera takes better pictures. I want to remember this trip and we haven't taken any yet."

"Whatever makes you happy." He smiled at me. I knew he thought I was being ridiculous, even if he didn't say it. He stepped toward me and wrapped his arms around my waist. "I've got plenty of memories of this trip, right up here." He tapped his forehead with his finger.

"Just humor me, okay?"

"I always do," he chuckled. "Come on, let's go. If you forgot something, I'll run back up and get it." He threw my bag over his shoulder and took me by the hand, leading me out to the beach.

We spent the last day of our trip on the beach. Chris and Tori joined us, with the same idea in mind. This was the last time the four of us would be together for a while. Tori and I laid out in the sun, while the guys threw the football back and forth.

I took his picture.

We walked down the beach, hand in hand. I stopped every now and then to pick up shells along the way. As an older couple walked by us, I stopped them and handed them my camera. They were more than happy to oblige.

They took our picture.

We sat on the beach, just talking and laughing. I put my feet next to his in the sand.

I took a picture.

When Ty fell asleep in the sun, I walked down by the water. In the wet sand, I drew a giant heart. I wrote our names in the heart with the date.

And I took a picture.

After his nap, Tyler and I waded out into the water. I wrapped my legs around him and he carried me out 'til the water came up to his chest. He kissed me passionately and ran his hands under my bikini, touching me in all the right places. Although I knew no one could see, I looked back to the beach to see if anyone was watching us. I saw Tori with my camera in her hand.

She took a picture.

By the end of the day, I had so many pictures I was sure it bordered on excessive. I didn't care. I didn't want to forget a single thing.

That night, we had our last bonfire on the beach. We all drank just a little too much, feeling buzzed but content. Shortly after the sun went down, Tori and Chris went back up to the house, no doubt for another round of marathon sex.

I was relaxed, sitting in Tyler's arms. I leaned my head back on his shoulder and looked into those bright blue eyes that mesmerized me. I whispered to him. "I think you promised me sex on the beach."

"Yeah. I did," he whispered back. He captured my lips and consumed me. The flames of the fire and the glow of the moon were our only light. He laid me back on the sand and made passionate love to me. It was slow and gentle and mind-numbing. We were trying to commit every detail of each other to memory, storing everything away for the times we would be apart.

When we had finished, Tyler grabbed a towel and covered us. We laid there holding each other in the firelight. We were in no hurry to return to reality. There was so much unspoken between us. Love. Hope. Fear. Pain.

We finally got dressed and gathered our things from the beach. I grabbed one of the empty water bottles and started scooping the sand, from where we had made love, into it.

"What are you doing, Ky?"

"This is sacred sand. I'm taking some of it home with me." This time Tyler didn't tease me or act like I was ridiculous. He kneeled down next to me, and scooped sand into the bottle with me.

That night we continued our love-making from the beach, in between the sheets. We took and gave unselfishly. I don't know how many times he brought me to pleasure, using his hands and mouth on every part of my body. We went well into the night before finally falling asleep in exhaustion.

I woke the next morning, snuggled tight in his arms, my head on his chest. This was the last time we would wake like this for a very long time. I placed soft kisses along his chest and ran my hand along his bare legs under the sheet. I moved my hand higher to rub his length. He began to harden in my hand, as I stroked him up and down. I kissed from his chest up to his soft lips. Although his eyes were still closed, his lips began to move with mine, as his hand ran along the curve of my back.

"One last time," I begged.

"Don't think of it that way. It's just for now. There will be many more times." He pushed my long hair out of my face and pierced me with those blue eyes. They were burning through me, reaching deep into my soul. Making promises.

He kissed my forehead and reached for a condom. I climbed on top of him and slid down. It was slow and sensual. I arched my back and closed my eyes, as I memorized the feeling of him inside me. I moved impossibly slow and rubbed myself along his hardness. He reached up and cupped my breasts, so soft and tender. With him still inside me, I leaned down on his chest and continued to move. Tyler lifted his hips into me, continuing our torturously slow pace. I wanted this to last forever. Our love making was emotionally driven. We didn't need words. Our bodies said everything that words couldn't.

# Chapter 32
## Tyler

Our drive home was somber. Kyla stayed snuggled into my side, with her head on my shoulder. I held her small hand and rubbed my thumb across her softness. We kept the radio low and talked about anything and everything, but me leaving for MSU. It was as if we didn't acknowledge it, it wouldn't be real. We could pretend for just a little longer that our lives were not about to change.

We pulled in her driveway, and I helped her carry everything into the house. She kissed me goodbye and promised to see me later that night. I did a lot of packing before we went on our trip, so that I could spend these last two nights with her. Two nights, that was all. How would I sleep without her wrapped in my arms, the heat of her warm little body next to me, her legs tangled with mine? It was going to be torturous.

That night, we went back to the park where it had all begun. I brought a blanket and laid it out on the grass. We laid on our backs, holding hands, staring up at the stars.

She spoke first, staring blankly at the sky. "Are you scared?" she whispered. "College football is way more intense than high school."

"A little," I admitted.

She turned her head and looked into my eyes. "You're going to be great, you know? I have faith in you. You can do this."

"What if I can't? It's a little intimidating."

"You can," she assured me. "Michigan State wouldn't have offered you the scholarship if they didn't believe it too. It's going to be hard at first, but I know you. You can do whatever you set your mind to."

"Are you giving me a pep talk?" I teased her.

She didn't smile back. Just looked at me thoughtfully. "Just telling the truth. I know how talented you are. I don't want our relationship to hold you back. I don't want to be a distraction. I'll always support you. And when you need me, I'll be here, waiting for you. I have your heart, remember?" She held up her hand, staring at the ring I put on her finger. "Just know, you're taking *my* heart with you. I'll always be by your side. I'm your biggest fan."

"You're my only fan, baby. Well, except for my parents."

"I'm being serious," she said quietly. "When everyone sees what you can do, you'll have lots of fans. But I'll always be your biggest."

I rolled over and hovered over her, resting my weight on my forearms. "I love you so much, Kyla. I don't know how I got so lucky to find you."

She reached her hands up and held my face. "It wasn't luck. It was fate. We were meant to be together. Always."

I kissed her then. Deep and passionate. This girl...no, woman... was everything to me. I would never find anything else as pure and perfect as her.

I made love to her that night, in that park, where it all began. I took her under the stars, for all the world to see.

The next day went by quickly, as I prepared to leave in the morning. God, I was glad I wasn't a chick. I let out a low laugh. I couldn't imagine all the things Kyla would be packing to take to Western with her. She had three bags just for our trip to the lake house. Being a guy was so much easier. Plus, I was coming back for a weekend in two weeks. I could grab anything I had forgotten, then.

Kyla got to my house later that evening. I brought her up to my room, so I could finish packing. She sat on my bed and watched me haphazardly throw stuff into a big duffle bag. I was going through one of my drawers when I found what I was looking for. I threw my high school football jersey at her. "I want you to have this."

She grabbed at the shirt I threw at her and shook it out to take a look. When she realized what it was, a big smile spread across her face. She ran her hands over my name on the back, then held it up to her face. "It smells like you," she said, breathing in the scent. "Thank you."

Kyla reached in her purse and pulled out a small package. "I've got something for you too." She held it out to me.

I sat down on the bed next to her and took the gift from her hands. I carefully pulled the paper back. "This is perfect." It was a silver frame, with a picture of us standing on the beach with the lake behind us. We had our arms around each other and I was looking down at her. Both of us had happy smiles on our faces as we looked at each other.

"I got our pictures developed today," she explained. "I had a hard time picking which picture to choose, so I tucked a couple of the others behind that one."

I turned the frame over and removed the back. I pulled the pictures out and looked at the first one. It was a picture of us kissing out in the water while I held her close. You could see the passion between us. Tori must have taken it. I'd have to thank her later. The next was a picture of the sand, where Kyla had drawn a perfect heart with our names in it. The last one took my

138

breath away. It was a picture of just Kyla. Her long, blond hair was blowing in the wind and her bright green eyes stared back at me. She was gorgeous. I was silent a long time just looking at that last picture.

"You don't have to put it out, if you don't want to. But maybe you could keep it in your desk drawer or something," she said nervously. "I don't know if it's really 'cool'," she finger-quoted, "to have a picture of your girlfriend on display. I don't want you to catch any crap for it."

"Ky, this is not going in a drawer. I don't care if I catch crap for it. I want to see your beautiful face every morning when I wake up." I reached my hand behind her head and pulled her into me, pressing her soft lips to mine. I looked in her eyes. "I'm not embarrassed of the fact that I love you. If anyone has the balls to say something, they can suck it."

Her lips turned up. "Suck it?"

"Yep!" I smiled back at her. "Do you care if I put the picture of you in the front?"

"They're yours to do with as you please," she said.

I rearranged the pictures, placing them back in the frame. I wrapped it one of my shirts and placed it in my duffle bag.

"I know you're going to be super busy with training and practice," she hesitated, "but will you try to call me at night? I just want to hear your voice."

"I'll call," I assured her. "You know… we can Skype too."

"Yeah." She narrowed her eyes at me. "Have you been talking to Tori?"

I reached up and grabbed the back of my neck nervously. "Chris, actually," I admitted.

"We'll Skype for sure." She glared at me. "As for the rest…we'll have to work up to that. Maybe we could start with sexting. Sound like a good compromise?"

I took her hands in mine. "We'll figure it out. I'm gonna miss you so fuckin' much."

The next morning, I got up at six and my dad helped me load up my car. I needed to check into my dorm and be at a team meeting by noon. This was it. I was nervous as hell, but excited too.

My parents had gotten me a refrigerator and a microwave. My mom bought me new sheets, a comforter, new pillows, and a shitload of towels. She had also packed me a tote full of miscellaneous stuff she thought I would need, including extra food. I had really only packed summer clothes and stuff to workout in. I would grab more clothes and anything else I needed when I came home in two weeks. My car was stuffed to the max.

"I feel weird sending you off by yourself," my dad stated. "We should be going with you."

"Dad, I told you, it's not that far. I'll have to start practice today, so it's not like we would get to hang out or anything anyways. I appreciate the offer, but I got this."

My mom hugged me tight. "You're so grownup now. It's hard to believe you don't need us anymore." A tear rolled down her face and she quickly wiped it away.

I hugged her back. "I'll always need you, but I can do this."

"How's Kyla dealing with you leaving?" she asked. "I'm going to miss seeing her. You two are practically attached at the hip."

"She's sad, but she's trying not to show it. Kyla's strong and she doesn't want to make this harder on me than it already is. But I'm going to miss her like crazy," I said.

"Do you think it's going to last with you two being at different schools?" my dad questioned.

"We're going to try like hell," I answered. "I can't imagine not being with her. She means the world to me." I looked at the time on my phone. "I really have to go. I promised Ky I'd stop by before leaving."

My mom pulled me in for one more hug. "I love you, honey. Be safe."

"I love you too, mom." I gave her a quick peck on the cheek.

"Call us if you need anything and call us when you get there," my dad instructed.

"Will do." I hugged my dad, then slipped into my car.

My mom looked so sad as I pulled out of the driveway. She waved her fingers at me and blew me a kiss.

I started off towards Kyla's house. It was my last stop before getting on the road.

I pulled into her driveway and she was sitting on the porch waiting for me. She walked out to my car and threw her arms around my neck. I grabbed her around the waist and pulled her in close, breathing in her scent once last time.

"You're going to be amazing," she whispered in my ear. She was my own personal cheerleader. "Call me tonight and let me know how everything goes."

She didn't cry or even tear up. She was being the strength I needed. "I will," I promised. "This is so hard…," I started.

She put her fingers over my lips to quiet me. "This is not goodbye. This is 'I'll see you soon'. I'll be right here waiting, just like I promised. Call me tonight," she said again.

I nodded my head, but I couldn't stop the tears that welled up in my own eyes. "Tonight," I said over the lump in my throat.

"Now, you better get going. I don't want you being late on the first day." She wrapped her arms around me and kissed me like there was no tomorrow. "I love you, Tyler Jackson."

"I love you too, Kyla O'Malley." I got in my car and started the engine. As I drove away from her house, I looked in the rearview mirror and saw her still standing at the bottom of the driveway, fading into the distance.

*There goes my heart.*

# Chapter 33
## Kyla

Saying goodbye to Tyler that morning was the hardest thing I've ever done. Especially after the week we just spent together. It was still early, so I crept back to my room.

My mom was standing at the top of the stairs waiting for me. "He's gone?" She questioned.

I just nodded my head, as tears filled my eyes. My mom pulled me into a tight embrace, giving me the support I needed. "I know it seems like the end, but it's only the beginning, sweetheart. He'll be back in two weeks, and soon after you'll be starting your own adventure. This is his."

"I know." I wiped the tears from my eyes. "I'm just going to miss him so much. I love him, mom."

"I know you do. And he loves you. You two will make it. I'm sure of it. You guys are so much like your father and I when we were young. This is just a little speed bump."

I hugged her tight. "Thanks, mom."

I laid down on my bed but couldn't fall back asleep. I looked around my room at all the memories of Tyler and me. Pictures were tucked into the corners of my mirror. My homecoming and prom corsages were hanging on the wall. Ticket stubs were scattered across my desk. And sitting next to my empty suitcase was that bottle of sand.

I wanted to take all these memories with me to school. I couldn't leave any of it behind. I went to my closet, not quite sure what I was searching for. I pulled out shoes, purses, and bunch of other crap. Sitting in the back of my closet was the purple photo box that I had been given for my birthday. I had never filled it with pictures since most of them were on my phone. This box would be perfect to store all our memories in. It was now officially the "Tyler and Kyla" box.

I started to collect the pictures from around my room and placed them in the box. I grabbed the movie tickets off my desk and the prom tickets from the drawer and placed them in the box. Everywhere I looked, I had stashed something. Love notes Tyler had written me, cards he had given me, more pictures… I placed them all in the box.

I went to my computer and uploaded all the pictures from my phone. I sent them to the corner drugstore to be printed out. I wasn't going to lose those if my phone decided to die on me.

I looked at the corsages hanging on the wall. What to do with those? I went down to the basement, not sure what I was looking for. My mom kept all kinds of crap down here, surely there would be something I could put them in. I dug around by the wrapping paper where I knew she kept all kinds of boxes. I found two small boxes that the corsages would fit into.

I turned off the light and started back toward the stairs when something caught my eye. Sitting on the top of a shelf were several glass bottles and jars. I flipped the light back on and grabbed a stool. Standing on the stool, I looked through all the bottles. Buried in the back, I found a small heart-shaped bottle with a cork. This would be perfect. I pulled it off the shelf and took it upstairs.

Once back in my room, I took the corsages off the wall and gently placed them in the small boxes. I took a purple Sharpie and wrote "Homecoming" on one and "Prom" on the other. I then searched around in the pocket of my suitcase and pulled out the shells I had collected from the beach. I dropped them into the heart-shaped bottle, just filling the bottom. I opened the bottle of sand from our last night on the beach and poured it on top of the shells. I pushed the cork in tight and placed it in the box, along with my corsages.

It was a start. I was sure I would find other things strewn around my room. But now, I had a place to keep everything. The past nine months had been the best of my life, and this photo box held all the evidence of that.

That night, I pulled Tyler's football jersey on and crawled into bed. It was still early, but he hadn't called yet. I downloaded a new book on my kindle, while I waited. I read for an hour and looked at the clock. It was a little after nine. He should have been back in his dorm by now. I picked up my phone and let my thumb hover over his name. *I will not call. I will not be that girl.* I put my phone back on my stomach and focused on my book. This was going to be a long two weeks, if I couldn't even handle one night.

9:45

Where the hell was he? Had he forgotten about me already? I went back to my book, but I was fighting against my eyelids. My eyes closed, and I startled myself awake.

10:15

Finally, I lost the battle and drifted off to sleep. I felt my phone buzz and my eyes popped open.

10:27

I looked at the screen and saw his face. I quickly answered. "Hey."

"Hey, baby." He sounded exhausted.

"How was your first day?"

"Brutal, but awesome. The guys are cool. The coach is a hard ass, though."

"It'll get better," I assured him. "How's your roommate?"

"Cody's cool. Listen, I'm sorry I called so late, but I have a feeling this is going to be the norm. I have to be back on the field by seven."

"Don't worry about it," I lied. "We knew this was going to be tough. I just wanted to hear your voice. I'm glad your first day went well."

"I miss you already," he admitted.

"I miss you, too." I stared at the ring on my finger. "Two weeks, baby, and I'll be back in your arms. It's not that long and I'm sure it's going to fly by for you. It sounds like they're going to keep you busy."

"I know you're right, but it just seems like forever right now. I love you, Kyla."

"I love you, too. You should get some rest. You've got a long day tomorrow."

"I'm so exhausted, it's going to take about two seconds to fall asleep."

"Go to bed. I'll talk to you tomorrow, okay?"

"Good night, baby."

"Good night." I ended the call and set my phone on my chest. This was going to be awful. The days might fly by for him, but mine were already dragging. Tomorrow I would go back to the marina to work. I hoped the distraction would help.

# Chapter 34
## Tyler

Practice at MSU was kicking my ass. Every day it was the same routine. Get up at six. Eat a quick breakfast and head to the gym. We were on weight training and cardio all morning. Then it was a quick lunch and onto the field, where we would do drills and run plays. Dinner. Watch tapes and go over more plays. We would finally finish around nine, then hit the showers and meet with the trainers who tended to any sore muscles or injuries. I had worked out during the summer, but you would never know it by what my body was being put through on a daily basis. But every day I handled it a little better. I was definitely increasing my strength and endurance.

By the time I got back to the dorm, it was usually around ten or so. I would make my nightly call to Kyla. It was my favorite time of the day. Just hearing her voice helped me get through the next day. She never whined about missing me or our time apart. She always had words of encouragement and support. I knew it was hard on her, but she never made me feel bad about it. Kyla was my rock.

I usually texted her in the morning, just to say 'good morning' and 'I love you'. She would send me sporadic texts throughout the day. They always put a smile on my face, just to know she was thinking of me.

My first two weeks quickly came to an end. All I could think of was getting home to my girl. We ended practice early

Friday and I was sitting on my bed packing my bag for the weekend.

"You going home to see your girl?" Cody asked as he plopped down on his bed.

"Yeah. It's been a long two weeks. You going home?" I asked.

"Nah. I'm just gonna hang around here. Catch up on my sleep," he answered.

"I'd love sleep, but I love my girl more," I said as I stood and grabbed my keys. "See ya Sunday night, man."

"See ya." He knuckle bumped me and I was gone.

I didn't even go home first. I went right to Kyla's house. Before I had the car turned off, she was running out the front door. I got out of the car and she jumped into my arms. I swung her around and locked my lips to hers. Fuck, she was a sight for sore eyes. Sure, I had my pictures, but nothing could replace the feel of her in my arms.

"God, I missed you, baby!" I wrapped my arms around her and held her tight to my chest.

"I'm so glad you're home. I missed you so much!"

I held her out so I could look at her beautiful face. Those green eyes always captivated me. "Would it be awful if I said I wanted to take you home with me right now? I need you. I need to be inside you," I whispered in her ear. My parents were a lot more liberal than Kyla's and let us spend time alone together in my room. Plus, I knew they were at a fund raiser tonight and wouldn't be back until late.

"It would be awful if you didn't say it. Please... let's go," she whispered back.

Kyla ran back to the house to grab her purse and talk to her parents. Then we were off. She snuggled into my side during the short drive. Just the scent of Kyla was intoxicating. The coconut that she always smelled like reminded me of the beach and our week at the lake house. The sex we'd had, her sleeping in my arms, waking to her every morning. She was my home.

148

I was afraid I wouldn't last long, but that would just be an excuse to have her again. We barely made it to my room before clothes were being torn off and thrown to the floor. In only my boxer briefs and Kyla in her bra and panties, I lifted her in my arms. She wrapped her legs around me, holding me tight. I carried her to the bed, setting her down on her back, as I leaned over her.

Kyla's hands ran up my chest. "What are they doing to you? You were sexy before, but my god, I swear your muscles have gotten even more defined in the last two weeks."

"I told you they were kicking my ass every day. I guess it must be paying off."

"Uh, yeah! I'd say it's definitely paying off." Kyla ran her hands over my shoulders and down my arms. I shuddered at her touch.

I ran my fingers down the side of face. She bent her head back giving me access to her neck. I kissed down her neck and between her breasts, down to her stomach. I pulled back and just looked at her. She had lust and need in her eyes. I'm sure I did too. I needed this girl like I needed air to breathe.

"I want to try something with you," her voice was quiet and unsure.

I quirked an eyebrow at her. "What do you have in mind?" I was more than willing to try anything with her. She was usually the one holding back, so I was curious. I wasn't complaining. Making love to Kyla was always more than satisfying, but we stayed in her comfort zone. I had made a promise to her that I would never push her into something she wasn't comfortable with, and I kept that promise. I had pushed the boundaries a few times, but she held all the cards. She was self-conscious and I found it endearing, so I wondered what was on her dirty little mind. If I'd learned one thing, it was that she had an inner sex kitten that she kept hidden, except with me.

"I'd rather show you than tell you," she said softly.

"Anything you want, baby," I assured her.

"Lay back on the bed for me." She didn't have to ask twice. Now I was intrigued.

I laid back on the bed. She got up and slid her panties down her legs, baring her freshly shaved pussy to me. I swallowed down my lust and let her drive this. Kyla climbed up on the bed and straddled my chest backward. She leaned forward and slipped her fingers in the waistband of my boxer briefs. I lifted my hips and she slid them down my legs. All the while, I had a perfect view of the curves down her back and ass.

I ran my hands up those curves and released the clasp of her bra. She let it fall down her arms and threw it to the floor. I reached for her tits from behind, ran my hands down her waist and rested them on the small of her back, making her arch more. She took my dick in her hands and gripped me hard, rubbing me up and down. She bent forward, taking me in her mouth and running her tongue along the top. Then she sunk down further 'til I was deep in her throat. She moved her hands and mouth in perfect rhythm. Stroking me. Sucking me. I let out a low growl and captured her hips in my hands.

I pulled her hips back toward me, until her pussy was at my mouth. She didn't protest, which told me that this is what she wanted. I loved her wetness right in my face. I stuck my tongue into her hot little pussy, lapping it all up. I moved my tongue through her folds to her clit and licked her up and down, all the while she was sucking me off so good. Her tongue wrapped around my dick as she took me to the back of her throat over and over again.

I licked her clit roughly, then took it into my mouth and sucked it in and out of my mouth. She released her mouth from me to let out an intense moan and savored her own pleasure. But what I was doing to her, made her take me again. She wrapped her lips around my dick and sucked harder and faster. I felt myself stiffen even more as she drove me closer to the edge. She was relentless, but so was I. I kept sucking her clit and dipped two fingers deep into her, pumping them in and out. I was gentle at first, but as she took me closer and closer to the brink of insanity, I thrust my fingers deeper and harder into her wetness. I licked and sucked her clit until I felt her pussy clamp down on my fingers.

With her mouth wrapped around my dick, I hardened and shuddered, releasing everything into her mouth, as she came on my face. She swallowed it all down as she sucked me through my orgasm, and I pumped her through hers. It was so intimate, so raw. She finally released me and moved her hips forward off my face. Her ass was glorious as it sat on my chest and she collapsed between my legs. I rubbed her ass and up to the small of her back again, as I caught my breath.

She peeked at me over her shoulder and I pushed her hair aside, so I could see her beautiful face. "I missed you so much, Kyla. That was…" I sighed, letting her know how awesome she had made me feel. Kyla turned and crawled up my chest, kissing me so deeply. We tasted ourselves on the other's tongues. It was erotic as fuck.

"That's not all I had in mind," she confessed, this time more brazen. She leaned to the side and whispered in my ear. "I want you to take me from behind." She dropped her head to the pillow next to me and buried her face. It was a huge step for Kyla to ask for what she wanted, unless we were in the heat of the moment. Then some of the shit that came out of her mouth shocked the hell out of me.

I turned my head to her ear and whispered back. "Yes. I would love to take you from behind."

She turned her head on the pillow. "Yeah?"

"Oh yeah." I could hardly contain the smile on my face. "Just give me a few to refuel."

We rolled on our sides, so we were face to face. I ran my knuckles down the side of her face then took her long strands and ran my fingers through them. "You know I'll do anything you want, right?" I asked her. "I feel like I can't get close enough to you. Being away from you has been torture."

"I hate being away from you. I want to make the most of every moment we have together. When I come to your games, do you think maybe I can stay the night with you? Do you think Cody would be alright with it?"

"I think that can be arranged." I ran my hand up her side, leaving goosebumps along her skin. I captured her lips with mine and kissed her deep and passionate. We devoured each other, feeding a hunger than couldn't be satisfied. We became a tangle of groping hands and twining legs. "Ready for round two?"

"Yes, I know this was my idea, but I'm a little nervous. We've never..." I put my finger to her lips.

"Don't overthink it. I got you, baby" I got on my knees and pulled her up to face me. I took her face in my hands. "Always together." I held Kyla close and then turned her by the shoulder, 'til her back was against my chest. She leaned forward, stretching like a cat, placing her hands on the bed. I ran my fingers along her soft back, pushing her tits to the mattress. Kyla went down on her forearms, sticking her beautiful, round ass in the air. "You are perfection," I said as I ran my hands along the curves of her. I nudged her legs apart with my knees. I took in the sight of her glistening, ready for me. I grabbed a condom and placed myself at her opening. Taking her hips, I pushed in gently, slow and deep. Kyla let out several short gasps as I sank into her warmth. Fuck, she was tight like this. I savored the feeling of her surrounding my cock, gripping me tightly.

"Tyler...I'm good. Please move, baby," she begged.

I slid out slowly and pushed back in at the same leisurely pace. God, I missed this. She pushed her hips back, grinding into me, encouraging me to move faster. "Fuck me harder!" I did. I picked up the pace, holding onto her hips tightly. Plunging deep into her pussy, over and over again.

Kyla's head dropped to the pillow as she let out muffled screams. I reached my hand around her waist and between her legs, providing the friction she needed to get off. I rubbed her clit furiously and I felt her walls clench me hard, pulsing around me.

It was enough to push me over the edge. I let out a low growl from deep in my chest and came inside her.

I leaned over her back, dropped my head next to hers and breathed her in. "Why have we never done that before?" she asked, gasping for breath. "I missed you so much." I collapsed beside Kyla and brought her head to rest on my chest. I held her tight, just enjoying the post-sex bliss.

"I missed you, too," I answered, running my fingers along her back.

I suddenly remembered the gifts I had brought her. I slid out from under her and quickly threw my jeans on.

"Where are you going?"

"I'll be back in a minute." I grabbed my keys, ran down the stairs and out to my car. I grabbed my duffle bag out of the trunk. When I got back to my bedroom, Kyla had snuggled under my blankets. She looked small and so adorable laying in my bed. "I brought you something." I unzipped the bag and pulled out two shirts. I threw them at her unsuspecting head. They landed on her face and she started to laugh, pulling them away.

"What's this?"

"Take a look."

She opened the first shirt. It was a green MSU football hoodie with JACKSON printed on the back. "I love it," she squealed. Then she shook open the other shirt. It was a MSU football jersey, also with my name on it.

"I want everyone to know when you come to the games that you're with me," I said giving her a devilish smirk. "Plus, I gotta show you off a little bit." I plopped down on the bed next to her.

"Maybe this will help keep those skanky bitches away from you." I laughed at her jealous side coming out. She threw the jersey over her head and stood up on the bed. It came down and hit her at mid-thigh. "How do I look?" she questioned, dancing around on the bed.

"Fucking adorable!" I scooted closer and looked up under the jersey at her beautiful naked body.

She held the fabric close against her legs. "Hey, no peeking!" she laughed.

"Oh, I'll peek all I want. You're all mine!" I reached up and grabbed her around the waist, pulling her back down to the bed with me. "Now everyone will know it." She looked so sexy in my jersey, her slender legs hanging out the bottom.

I made love to her wearing nothing but my jersey.

We got dressed and snuggled up on my bed together. God, I'd missed this. It didn't take long for us to fall asleep in each other's arms.

I was shaken awake by a hand on my shoulder. I looked down at Kyla sleeping and then looked up at my dad.

"I just wanted to let you know we were home. Is Kyla spending the night?" he whispered. My parents were cool. They knew Kyla and I were having sex, but they didn't seem to mind us spending time together in my room.

I rubbed at my eyes. "I don't think her dad would like that very much," I answered. "What time is it?"

"It's a little after midnight."

"Thanks, dad. I'll take her home in a bit. I just want to hold her for a while longer. I really missed her."

He smiled down on me. "I know you did. Don't fall back asleep or you'll be in hot water with her parents."

"Okay."

My dad quietly left, leaving me alone with my girl. I brushed the hair away from her face and placed a gentle kiss on her forehead. She was my angel. I knew us being apart was going to be hard, but I wasn't ever going to let her go.

# Chapter 35
## Kyla

*December of our Junior Year in College*

We'd made it! It wasn't easy, but Tyler and I made it! Football season was tough, but I went to every home game, and some away games, if they weren't too far. I would spend the night with him, after each game, locked tight in his arms. Luckily, Cody was cool. He usually went to a party after the games. Tyler and I mostly passed on the parties, and so we got our time alone together. After football season, things relaxed considerably, and Tyler would have time to visit me at Western. On those nights, Tori would go stay in Chris's room so we could have our alone time.

I was right about some things. Tyler was amazing. I knew he would be. His freshman year, he was the backup quarterback. He proved himself over and over again. He had a gift. He had a way of seeing the field and knowing just where to put the ball. By sophomore year, he had taken over the quarterback position outright. Tori and Chris usually came to the games with me, but I was his biggest fan. I cheered so loud, that my voice would go hoarse by the end of every game. I wore his name on my back proudly and waited for him by the locker room after every game. He was always so pumped after a game, and our best sex happened on those nights.

I was right about the skanky bitches, too. They flocked around Tyler like he was a superstar. I guess he was. He had gotten more filled out, as he got older. He had the body of a god and the looks to go with it. His dark hair and blue eyes were a deadly combination. The girls…skanky bitches…fell over their own feet to get to him. They flirted shamelessly and acted utterly ridiculous, throwing themselves at him. I always stood off to the side and watched their embarrassing display of want and lust. But Tyler never paid any attention to them. When he came out of the locker room, he would push right by the flock of girls calling his name, walk right into my arms, and kiss me passionately for all of them to see. Sometimes, when I was being catty, I would turn and wave over my shoulder to the hoard of skanks, as we walked away with our arms locked around each other.

On the nights we did decide to go to a party, the girls were even worse. They pretended like I didn't exist. Girls would come up to congratulate Tyler on a game, hanging on his arm or rubbing their hands on his chest. It was sickening. Tyler simply said thanks and moved along. If we were dancing, the girls would squeeze right between us and try rocking against his body. Tyler was skilled at maneuvering around them and bringing me back into his arms. I still didn't trust them. But I completely trusted Tyler. He had never given me a reason not to.

Honestly, I hated going to the parties at MSU but sometimes it was necessary. The guys were cool with me though and accepted me as a part of Tyler's life. They were never disrespectful, probably because they knew how protective Tyler was of me. Freshman year, some guy tried to put the moves on me, groping my ass and acting like a drunken idiot. Tyler knocked him out cold with one punch. He was easy going, until someone messed with me. Then he transformed into my protective Rottweiler. Nobody wanted to cross that line. And I was fine with that.

Our relationship was solid. We had made things work, even though the conditions were not ideal. I kept to my promise and always supported Tyler. I knew he had so much talent. The pro scouts were already sniffing around, and he had a real chance at playing for the NFL. This was his dream, and I would never stand in the way of that. I had my own dreams, but they paled in comparison to his. I just hoped that I would be able to put my artistic skills to good use and find a job I loved. That's why, even though I could have done anything, I chose graphic arts and advertising. I was sure it was a career path that would allow me to do what I had a natural talent for.

One thing about going to all the games, was how fast the fall semester flew by. Tyler and the guys made it to the Rose Bowl for the first time in over twenty-five years. To say the energy on campus was electric would be an understatement. Everyone was totally pumped. They'd be playing against Stanford on New Year's Day.

Tyler and I went home for Christmas break. We spent a lot of time with our families, but plenty of time alone together too. My family was his and his was mine. After three years, we'd become inseparable. I couldn't imagine it any other way.

I'd been a little off lately though. I'd been dealing with some issues that I really needed to talk to Tyler about, but now was not the time. With the Rose Bowl looming, I didn't want to be a distraction. I plastered a smile on my face and pretended that everything was great. Tyler didn't seem to notice, so I guess my acting skills were actually pretty good. I promised myself that I'd talk to him when the bowl game was over.

# Chapter 36
## Tyler

Life was pretty awesome right now. I had my girl. I was the QB for MSU. And we were going to be playing in the Rose Bowl.

Kyla had been more than I could have ever dreamed of. I wanted everything to work for us when we went away to college, but I would be lying if I didn't say that the distance had made me nervous. Football season was a crazy, busy time. Between practice, games, and classes, there was very little time for anything else. Kyla came to all my games, and as she promised, she was my biggest fan. She would bring Chris and Tori or sit with my parents. She proudly wore my name on her back and cheered louder than anyone else.

I loved the games. The roar of the crowd. The energy in the stadium. The feeling of winning. But my favorite time was always after the games, when I could take Kyla back to my room and make love to her.

She was right though; the girls here were ruthless. They were always trying to get my attention. I'd had more than a few offers for no-strings attached sex. The temptations were there. It would have been easy to say yes and think that she would never know. But I never did. What Kyla and I had, wasn't worth destroying for a one-night fuck. I wanted to marry that girl one day and I was not about to mess that up. She was my everything.

I'd had my worries about her too. I knew that the guys at Western must have be hitting on her. She was smart, sexy, and gorgeous. I'd asked Chris if I had anything to worry about. He said she was busy with her classes and spent a lot of time in her dorm room studying. He said he'd never seen anything that I should be worried about. She was totally devoted to me. Deep down I knew nothing would happen, but I was a guy and I knew how other guys thought.

Kyla and I came home for Christmas break. We were able to spend a ton of time together and that was a nice change from our weekends only routine. I had to go back to MSU early to be with the team and get ready to fly across the country. January first we played in Pasadena against Stanford. I was totally stoked. Kyla, Tori, Chris and my parents would be flying out a few days later. They had tickets to come out for the game and I was able to get them awesome seats. I was so glad my girl, my friends, and my family would be there.

Tonight was my last night with Kyla before leaving. I just wanted to spend some time with my girl.

# Chapter 37
## Kyla

"What do you want to do tonight, baby?" Tyler took my hand and kissed it. We were sitting in his car, and it was freaking freezing out. That was the thing about Michigan. The summers were great, but the winters could be brutal.

"Can we go back to your house? Maybe we can watch a movie or something. I just want to be snuggled up next to you." We didn't get very much time to just be. Seeing each other only on weekends, made everything rushed because we knew we only had a short time together. I liked spending time at Tyler's because his parents were rarely home and when they were, nobody worried about what we were doing. They were VERY liberal. My parents were more conservative, and my dad was always checking on us.

"Whatever you want. That actually sounds really good, we haven't had a lot of downtime lately." Tyler pulled out of the driveway and headed toward his house. I rested my head on his shoulder and closed my eyes. I'd been exhausted and right now this felt nice. I took in the smell of his cologne and just relaxed.

When we got to Tyler's, no one was home. We went right up to his room and shut the door. I stripped off my winter coat and shoes and plopped down on his bed. Tyler plopped next to me and wrapped his arm around my shoulders. I snuggled my head to his chest. I loved these moments where it just us, with no outside distractions.

"You know I love you, right?" Tyler's question took me by surprise.

I turned my head so I could look in his deep blue eyes. "Of course, I know you love me. Why would you ask me that?"

He ran his hand through my hair. "I just know that this has been hard on you. Football season is so busy, and I feel like I don't spend enough time with you. With the Rose Bowl coming, it's taken even more time from us."

I glanced down at the heart shaped ring on my finger. I never took it off. Ever. "Ty, we knew it was going to be like this. After the Rose Bowl, things will get easier. I know it's a juggling act for you and it's not easy. I promised I would always support you and I will. I'm not going anywhere." Yes, it had been hard on me too, but wouldn't trade it for anything.

Tyler kissed my forehead and stared at me intently. "I don't want you to ever think that you come second to football. I'd give it all up if you asked me to."

"I'd never ask you to do that. You have an amazing talent. I wouldn't be surprised if you got drafted by the NFL. That would be pretty cool, don't you think?" I said with a big smile.

"Yeah," he smiled. "That would be pretty awesome." I saw a glimmer in his eye as he pondered the possibility. But then, he turned serious again. "It wouldn't mean anything without you though. I *am* going to marry you someday. I bet we'd make some pretty babies together. You're going to be adorable when you're pregnant." He ran his knuckles down the side of my face, then grabbed my chin and pulled it to him for a kiss.

I swallowed down the lump in my throat. We'd talked about marriage before, but this is the first time he'd ever said anything about having a baby. I wanted all of it. Everything he'd just said, made my heart melt. "Where is all this coming from?"

"My heart. I never want you to forget how important you are to me. It seems like finishing college is going to take forever. I don't know if I can wait that long."

He had made me so happy. He couldn't have said anything more perfect tonight. "Let's get through the bowl game first and then we can talk about this more. I mean, we could make it work right? I could transfer to MSU and we could get an apartment. Or maybe we could find someplace in between."

"We could definitely make it work." Tyler gave me that panty dropping smile and kissed me deeply.

I ran my hands up under his shirt and traced his muscles with my fingertips. I placed gentle kisses down his stomach and started to unbutton his jeans. I unzipped them and kissed down that sexy "V". He lifted his hips and pushed his jeans down his legs. I pulled his boxer briefs down, letting him spring free. I wrapped my hand around him and began rubbing him up and down. I bent forward and took him in my mouth. I took him deep to the back of my throat and swirled my tongue around the head. Tyler let out a low growl and pushed my hair out of the way, so he could watch. "I love seeing your mouth wrapped around my dick. You are so fucking sexy." I pushed him deeper into my throat, rubbing his head along the roof of my mouth on the way down. Tyler started to pump his hips up and down, helping to set the rhythm. I felt him harden more and twitch. "I'm gonna come, baby." He emptied everything he had into my mouth and I swallowed down every last drop.

Tyler grabbed me under the arms and pulled me up to him. I kissed him with all I had. I poured all my love into that kiss. He was my other half and I needed him like I needed air. I broke the kiss and whispered to him. "I love you so much, Ty." I got tears in my eyes. I tried to blink them back, but they fell down my cheeks.

"I love you too, Ky. Why are you crying?" He wiped my tears away with his thumb and looked at me with concern in his eyes.

I shrugged. "I don't know. Guess I'm just feeling emotional."

He wrapped his arms around me tightly and held me to his chest. He kissed the top of my head and buried his face in my hair. "I'm gonna take care of you. Always." We stayed like that for a long time. Just buried in the warmth of each other.

Tyler broke the silence. "I think it's your turn." He rolled me onto my back and pulled his shirt off. Then he lifted mine over my head. He ran his hands over my bra, rubbing my nipples through the lace. I arched my back and he reached behind me and undid the clasp. He pulled the straps of my bra down my arms and tossed it to the side. He ran his hands over my breasts. "You are so beautiful." He leaned down and took one of my breasts into his mouth, sucking and nipping gently with his teeth. Then he did the same to the other. I swear his mouth was magic. I let out a moan of pleasure.

Tyler slid his hands down my flat stomach and to my jeans. He removed my pants and panties in one motion, pulling them down my legs. He ran his hands back up the inside of my legs to my thighs and gently pushed them apart. His head disappeared between my thighs as he worshipped my body. His tongue darted out and licked at my opening. I was so wet already. He ate me out like a starving man. Then his tongue moved up through my folds to my clit. He licked me up and down and then sucked the sensitive nub into his mouth. He knew it drove me insane. He stuck two fingers inside me, pumping them in and out, as he continued his assault on my pussy. My hips started to buck up off the bed at the pleasure he was giving me. He placed a hand on my stomach to keep me still and continued to suck. I threw my head back and let out a strangled moan. I was being wound so tight, as I climbed higher and higher. And then, white lights flashed behind my eyelids as I shattered beneath Tyler's tongue. "Holy fuck!" I breathed out, trying to catch my breath.

Tyler crawled up my body. "I never get tired of seeing you like this. You are so beautiful when you come." He tangled his tongue with mine and I tasted myself. It was so erotic.

"Make love to me, Ty." I begged him softly as I ran my hands through his hair.

He reached into the drawer for a condom, and I grabbed his wrist. "I don't wanna use one," I said. "I just want to feel you, and only you, inside me."

He looked at me warily. "You're killing me, Ky. Do you know how tempting that is?"

"Please," I begged. "Just this once." I needed this. I needed the connection.

Tyler contemplated, then sighed as he looked at me. "I'm pulling out. I'm not gonna come inside you." He was setting the conditions.

"Okay," I agreed. "Please... I just need to feel you." I knew I sounded desperate, and I was.

Tyler settled back over me. He threaded his fingers with mine and brought my hands above my head, so they rested on the pillow. "You're crazy, you know that?" he whispered in my ear.

"Crazy in love." I smiled up at him. Our eyes connected as I opened my legs for him. "Make love to me," I whispered.

He gently placed his tip at my entrance and hissed at the contact. I was so wet and ready for him. He pushed in slowly and his eyes rolled back as he leaned his head back. "Oh my god."

I felt all of him, as he slowly pushed forward. The hard and the soft. His size stretched me wide, filling me completely. Every ridge, every movement. He pushed in so deep, I could feel him pushing against my cervix. He slowly pulled back and slowly pushed back in. It was a delicious combination of pleasure and torture twisted together.

Tyler put his hands behind my thighs and pressed them to my chest. I went up on my elbows and pushed myself up to my hands. I kissed Tyler deeply, "I wanna see you inside me." We both watched as he disappeared inside me over and over again, stretching me to accommodate his width. It was, without a doubt, the most intimate moment we had ever shared. I reached down and rubbed my clit. I was so turned on, that it only took a couple strokes of my fingers to push me over the edge. I started to pulse around Tyler's dick, squeezing him tightly with my muscles. He hissed loudly, pumped two more times and pulled out. Hot streams of cum, poured onto my stomach. I watched as he emptied himself on me. "That was so fuckin' hot," I exclaimed as I laid back on the bed.

"Yeah? Which part?" he asked as he collapsed beside me.

"All of it. Watching you fuck me. Seeing your dick disappear into my pussy. Watching you come. All of it."

"You've got a dirty mouth, you know that?" he teased me.

"Only around you. And I think you secretly love it." I teased back.

"It's not really a secret." He tapped the tip of my nose. "I do love it. It's going to kill me to go back to using a condom after that."

I closed my eyes, laid on Tyler's chest, and enjoyed the moment. Holding each other. No distractions. No worries. Just us.

# Chapter 38
## Tyler

It was game day! This stadium was amazing. The energy was electric. It felt surreal to be playing in the Rose Bowl. Not many players ever got this chance. Win or lose, it didn't matter.

Okay, that was a lie. I lived to win. Everyone would be watching, including the pro scouts. This game could help solidify my future.

My parents had flown in yesterday. I knew Kyla, Tori, and Chris were here too, they had flown in this morning. I got a text from Kyla, asking if she could see me before the game. I told her to meet me outside the locker room. I would let security know she was coming. I was waiting for her now. I had to see my girl before the biggest game of my life. I was going through my phone, looking for the music that always pumped me up before every game. I had my ear buds in and pushed play, turning Godsmack up and feeling the energy move through my veins.

I was so into the music, that I didn't see her approach. She wrapped her arms around my neck, went up on her tip toes, and collided her mouth with mine. I pulled the ear buds out and wrapped her in my arms. "I'm so glad you're here," I spoke into her hair. "I couldn't do this without you."

"You could, but you don't have to." She flashed a smile at me. "How are you doing? Are you nervous?"

"A little bit, but seeing you helps."

"Don't be nervous. You're going to be amazing! Just do your thing. It's just another game. When you get on the field, it's you and your team. Forget about the crowd. Forget about the cameras."

"God, I love you. You're my anchor." I gave her one more soul searing kiss.

Coach came out of the locker room looking for me. "Jackson, let's go. Game time!"

"Coming, Coach," I answered over my shoulder. I turned back to Kyla. "I gotta go. I'll see you after the game. Meet me back here?"

"You know it, baby. I love you. Oh, and not that you'll need it, but…good luck!"

I tapped her on the ass and went into the locker room. Cody was sitting on the bench by my locker. "Where were you?" he questioned.

"Just had to see Kyla before the game," I answered.

"Don't you ever get enough of her?" He smirked at me.

"Nope! I'm gonna marry that girl one day." I sat down next to him, resting my arms on my knees.

"Dude, do you even know how lucky you are? It's cool that she came all the way to Pasadena for you. When I first met you, I thought you were totally pussy whipped. And you are… but she's worth it."

"Yeah, she is." I let out a big breath and turned to Cody. He'd become like a brother to me over the last couple of years. "I'm proposing to her when we get back home." He probably thought I was nuts.

"No shit! Congratulations, man!" He pulled me into a big bear hug and patted me on the back.

"You don't think it's crazy?" I asked.

"It's totally crazy! But you guys have been together for three years, right?"

I nodded my head.

"It's cool. You guys were made for each other."

167

The first half had just ended and were up by fourteen. I could hear Kyla cheering for me. She really was my biggest fan.

We were sitting in the locker room along the benches, as Coach gave his halftime speech. I dropped my head. All I could think about, was that ring sitting in the drawer of my desk.

Cody knocked me on the back. "You alright, man?"

I looked up at him. "I'm good." I dropped my head again.

I heard Coach call my name. "Jackson, how's your arm? You good for the second half?"

I gave him a thumbs up and he nodded at me. Whenever I got on the field, a sense of calm took over. I was focused. I threw the ball like a laser, knowing just where to put it.

I drifted off again in my own thoughts but came back when I heard the end of Coach's speech. "Get your asses out there and let's take this home boys!" Everyone was hopped up on adrenaline and testosterone. The sounds of hooting and hollering were deafening in the small space of the tunnel coming out of the locker room. We made our entrance back on the field, and the crowd went wild.

As the clock ticked down, I knew we had this game. We ran a few short plays, using up as much time between each one as possible. We were down to a few seconds. Our center snapped the ball to me, and I took a knee, effectively running down the clock and winning the game, twenty-four to twenty.

The crowd went crazy. The whole team ran onto the field, and it was complete chaos. While I was high fiving and hugging it out with the guys, I saw my little blond cheerleader running across the field to me. I broke from the guys and held my arms out for her. She jumped up into them and I swung her around. I was sweaty as hell and probably stunk, but she didn't care.

"Congratulations, baby! I knew you could do it!" Her smile lit up her face. "I'm so proud of you!"

I pulled her in tight and she wrapped her legs around my waist. She weighed practically nothing, and I loved holding her like this. I kissed her hard and set her back on her feet. "Thanks, Ky!" I threw my arm over her shoulder and we walked off the field. "You don't know how much it meant to me for you to be here. There's no one I would rather share this with."

We got closer to the locker rooms, and found Tori and Chris waiting for us. Tori threw her arms around my neck and gave me a huge hug. "Congratulations!" Chris gave me the one-armed man hug, patting me on the back. "Great game, man!"

"Thanks! I'm so glad you guys flew out for this. It means the world to me."

"We couldn't let Kyla fly out by herself." Tori smirked. "Plus, this guy," she pointed over her shoulder to Chris, "is living vicariously through you. We wouldn't have missed it."

"There's a huge celebration party on campus tomorrow. You guys are coming, right?"

"We'll be there." Chris fist bumped me. "Think it'd be cool if we crash in your dorm?"

"Yeah, no problem. I'll text you guys the address for the party. I gotta be there early, so I'll just meet you at the party."

"Cool, man." Chris turned to Kyla. "I hate to break up the love fest, but we need to start heading back to the hotel so we can catch our flight. We'll meet you up on the concourse?"

"Sure," Kyla answered. "Just give me a couple of minutes."

Chris and Tori started walking up the steps, giving us a few more minutes alone. "I wish we were going home together," I said, pressing my forehead to hers.

"I know, me too. But I'll see you tomorrow. And the next day." She gave me a mischievous look. "Now that football's over, we'll have more time together."

I picked her up one more time and swung her around. She squealed like a little girl. Her laughter was infectious. "I'm looking forward to it. I love you, baby. I'll see you tomorrow."

"I love you, too. See you tomorrow." I gave her one final kiss and patted her on the ass, sending her up to meet Chris and Tori. As I watched her go up the steps, all I could think about was how lucky I was, and the ring waiting at home. I made up my mind right there, that I would propose to her the day after the party. In two days she would be my fiancé.

# Chapter 39
## Kyla

We flew back to Michigan and then drove to campus. By the time we arrived we were all so tired that we immediately fell asleep. All I could think about was seeing Ty at the party, and hopefully doing some serious talking the next day. Now that the Rose Bowl was over, I couldn't put this off any longer.

I spent extra time getting myself ready for the party. Tyler was the hometown hero and I wanted to make sure I looked good for him. Plus, I needed to make a statement to the skanky bitches that I wasn't fooling around. He was mine. Tori helped me curl me hair in soft waves that flowed down my back. I went a little darker with my makeup, and I could honestly say I looked sexy. I threw on a pair of skinny jeans, a tight black top that showed off my boobs, and my tall black boots.

"You look hot!" Tori exclaimed as she looked me over.

"I just want to look extra sexy for him tonight," I sighed. "He's kind of a big deal and I want him to be proud to be with me."

She sat back on my bed and rolled her eyes at me. "I don't know what you're worried about. That boy would think you were sexy if you wore a paper bag."

I sat down next to her and grabbed her hands. I didn't know how she would take what I was going to say next. "I know." I sighed and dug deep for my courage. "Things are changing though. You know how hard this has been with the two of us being so far apart. Weekends come and go so fast. I need more. He needs more."

"Okaaaay... you're starting to scare me a little bit. What's your point?"

"The point is…" I closed my eyes and blurted it out. "I'm thinking of transferring to MSU in the fall so we can get an apartment together."

Tori's eyes widened in shock. "You're ditching me? What about your graphic arts degree? They don't have that same type of program at MSU." She looked hurt. We had always planned on being roommates. This was supposed to be our experience together.

"I'm not ditching you! I have to follow my heart. Can you imagine not seeing Chris every day? It's so damn hard and it's not getting any easier."

She scowled at me. "No, I can't imagine not seeing Chris every day. It would break me."

"And I don't want it to break Tyler and me. He can't transfer. Not with him being the QB. It would end any chance of him going pro. I can't take that away from him."

Tori's eyes softened with her next words. "I get it. But I'm still going to see you right?"

I hugged her tight. "Of course. A little distance can't break our friendship. We've been through way too much together. I'm still going to need you."

I felt lighter now that I had broken the news to Tori. Tyler and I still had a lot of details to work out, but I was excited about the thought of us living together. It would make EVERYTHING so much easier. I just hoped he would be as excited as I was.

We packed into Chris's truck and headed to MSU for the big celebration. The weather turned bad. A snowstorm rolled in about a half hour into our trip. The blizzard made it almost impossible to see and traffic was moving at a snail's pace.

"Fuck!" Chris let out his frustration. "This fucking sucks! I'm so glad we're not coming back home tonight. I'm going to be done with driving by the time we get there."

I felt bad because I knew if it wasn't for me, we wouldn't be driving in this weather. It was coming down so hard that it was practically a white out. "I'm sorry. I feel bad that you guys are doing this for me. We can go back if you want to. I'll just text Tyler and let him know what's going on."

"No, it's fine. Hopefully, this will let up soon. We'll go and have some drinks. All's good," Chris reassured me.

"Are you sure?" I asked.

Tori turned around and leaned over the seat. "Kyla, relax. It's fine. We want to be there for Tyler too. This is a big deal. You have to be there."

"I know, but I still feel bad. You guys are the best. I don't know what I would do without you two. Thank you for helping me get through all of this."

Chris looked into the rearview mirror and caught my eye. "Hey, baby girl, you know we love you right? You're not putting us out. You're kind of like a baby sister to me."

"Thanks, Chris. I love you guys too. But you do know we're the same age, right?"

"Yeah, but that doesn't stop me from feeling protective over you. I promised Ty I would watch over you and I'm not going back on that."

I sat back and let out a little huff. "You guys really are the best. Thanks."

Tori gave me a wink. "Now sit your sexy ass back, and just let Chris handle this. We'll be there soon, and then we can all get our drink on!"

# Chapter 40
## Tyler

Where the hell were they? They should have been here by now.

Cody came up and clapped me on the back of the shoulder. "Dude, relax. She'll be here. I heard there's a snowstorm coming. She's probably just stuck in traffic." He led me over to the makeshift bar where a bunch of the guys from the team were standing. "In the meantime, let's do some fucking shots! We've got some celebrating to do!"

He had a point. We were supposed to be celebrating. I knew Kyla would get there when she could. I wasn't a huge drinker, but what the hell? I'd already had a few beers and was feeling a little buzzed. I grabbed a vodka off the bar and raised my glass to my teammates. "To kickin' ass at the Rose Bowl!" I shouted. Everyone raised their glasses and threw back their shots.

A few shots later and I was feeling pretty good. Hell, who was I fooling? I was fucking drunk. I hadn't been this drunk in…well ever. My vision was a little blurry and I wasn't so steady on my feet, but I was having a good time. I needed this. I'd been wound so tight lately that I just needed the release.

The bass of the music thumped, and people were everywhere. The dance floor was crowded with couples rocking against each other. I even saw a few trying to hide the fact that they were fucking on the couch. Apparently, anything went tonight. I missed my girl.

I headed to the bathroom and opened the door. I interrupted one of my teammates getting a blow job from one of the cheerleaders. I muttered my apologies, shut the door, and looked for another bathroom.

I stumbled down the hall and finally found one. Thankfully, this one was empty. I went in and took a piss. Then I looked at myself in the mirror. My eyes were glassy, and I was having a hard time focusing. Kyla was going to be so irritated with me. Where the hell was she anyway?

I made my way back to the crowd and spotted the back of her across the room. Her long, blond hair was hanging down in soft waves. I felt my dick harden at the sight of her. I had to have her right now. I needed to be inside my girl!

I walked up behind her and grabbed her hand. I turned around and led her up the stairs, pulling her behind me. I found an empty room. I didn't bother to turn the lights on. I could barely see her in the shadows. We didn't say a word as we stripped our clothes off and made our way to the bed. I pushed her back on the mattress. "I want you, baby," I slurred.

She scooted up the mattress and spread her legs for me. I found a condom in my jeans that were now at my feet, and wasted no time rolling it on. I crawled up the bed and stuck my dick in her hot little pussy. "Baby, I'm so sorry. I'm so fucking drunk, but I just had to have you right now."

She moaned out in pleasured as I pounded into her over and over again.

# Chapter 41
## Kyla

Thank god we were finally there. That drive took forever. I'd been trying to text and call Tyler, but he hadn't answered. We got inside, and I instantly knew why he hadn't answered my calls. The bass was thumping, and the music was blasting so loud that you could barely hear yourself think.

I leaned over and yelled in Tori's ear, "I'm going to try to find Tyler."

She gave me a thumbs up. "Chris and I are going to go check out the bar," she yelled back.

I gave her a thumbs up in return and started my search. I was trying to push my way between people, but this place was so crowded. Since I was short it was hard to see anything even with my tall boots on.

I pushed a few people out of my way, and I finally saw Cody standing with a group of guys. I made my way over to him and tapped him on the shoulder. I yelled up to him, "Have you seen Tyler?"

His eyes went wide. He leaned down to my ear. "Hey, Kyla. I think I saw him go upstairs, let me go see if I can find him."

"That's okay. I can go look," I said.

"No, really, I'll go," Cody insisted.

What the fuck! I looked over at the stairs and then back at Cody who had a guilty look on his face. "What the hell is going on, Cody?" When he didn't answer, I stormed over to the stairs and started running up them. Cody was quick to follow.

He grabbed my arm. "Seriously, Kyla, this isn't a good idea. I'll find him."

I shook his arm off and continued up the stairs. All the while, Cody was pleading with me to stop. When I got to the top, I turned and crossed my arms over my chest. I narrowed my eyes at him. "Don't you dare try to protect him!" I yelled over the music.

I was starting to hyperventilate. This was not good! Obviously, Cody knew something I didn't. I rushed down the hallway, banging on doors and yelling his name, "Tyler! Tyler, where the fuck are you!" I tried to open some of the doors, but most were locked. I got to the end of the hallway and put my hand on the last doorknob.

Cody reached for my arm. "Kyla, don't. Just don't. He's drunk. It's my fault!"

I pushed his chest back with both hands, using every bit of strength I had. I opened the door and got the shock of my life.

I heard Tyler's voice clear as day, "Shut the fucking door! Somebody's in here!"

I stood there, with my hands over my mouth. I saw his naked body laying over some equally naked chick. His dick was deep inside her.

# Chapter 42
## Tyler

I was deep inside my girl when the door swung open. Why the fuck didn't I lock it? I yelled out, "Shut the fucking door! Somebody's in here!"

The light from the hall flooded across the bed. I tried to shield her, as I looked toward the door. Standing in the doorway was Kyla. Her eyes were wide, and her hands were covering her mouth.

"Kyla?"

I looked down at the girl beneath me. I looked in her eyes. Blue. Not green. "It's actually Madison," she giggled. I sobered up really quick at the realization.

I jumped off the bed. Kyla turned and ran down the hallway. "Kyla, stop!" I screamed. I quickly found my jeans and tried to pull them on, almost falling over in the process. Once I got them pulled up, I ran from the room. No shirt. No shoes. I ran down the stairs. I saw her blond hair rush out the front door as it slammed shut. I got to the door and opened it, only to see her running down the sidewalk. "Kyla, come back!"

I nearly fell over as I got pushed to the side. Tori was running after her.

"FUCK!" I screamed out. *WHAT THE FUCK HAVE I DONE?*

# Chapter 43
## Kyla

I ran down the stairs as fast as I could, nearly falling over anyone who was in the way. I rushed out the front door and ran down the sidewalk. I could hear Tyler calling to me. The snow fell heavily, and the cold air bit at my skin. I didn't care. I just kept running, trying to put as much distance between what I had seen and myself.

I don't know how far I ran before I collapsed into the snow. I threw my hands over my head and let out a gut-wrenching scream into the cold, dark night. "Nooooo!" Finally, I just started sobbing right there on the sidewalk. The tears came fast, there was no controlling them. It was the ugliest cry I had ever done. I was so broken!

Suddenly, warm arms were around me, hugging me close. "Kyla, what happened?" It was Tori. She cradled me into her and rubbed my back. I just kept sobbing. I couldn't get the words past the lump in my throat.

Tori continued to hold me. I looked up at her, as the tears streamed down my face. "He was fucking someone else," I choked out.

"No!" she exclaimed in disbelief.

I nodded my head.

"Oh Kyla! I'm so sorry." She just held me.

I continued to cry. My legs were soaked from kneeling and my wet hair hung in my face, as the snow continued to fall down on us. I hugged Tori tight and cried on her shoulder. "That's not even the worst part," I said quietly.

Tori held me out at arm's length and watched me crumble before her. "What do you mean, that's not the worst part?" she questioned.

I looked her in the eye and revealed the secret I'd been holding onto for the last few weeks. "I'm pregnant!"

**Kyla and Tyler's story continues in *Shattered Hearts…***

*Kyla~*
One secret.
One lie.
Can he forgive me? Or will this be the end of us?

*Tyler~*
One night.
One mistake.
Can she forgive me? Or will this be the end of us?

As Kyla's life spirals out of control, she desperately seeks the one thing that can hold her together. Her lies continue to haunt her, and it seems there is no redemption. She's searching for something to be right again and finally she's found it. But is it really what she needs or is she just grasping at anything to find happiness?

As Tyler comes to terms with reality, he desperately seeks anything that can hold him together. His mistakes haunt him, and he'll do whatever it takes to erase her from his memory. He's searching for something to ease his pain and seeks it in all the wrong places. When he realizes what he truly needs, will it be too late, or has he pushed her too far?

Their hearts have been shattered and their lives forever changed. Only time will tell if they can put the pieces back together. Kyla's and Tyler's story continues as they face the destruction they have brought upon themselves.

# Acknowledgments

To my husband~ I could have never done this without your love and support. Thank you for putting up with my endless hours of writing, all the take-out dinners, and my never-ending questions about football. I know I made you crazy, but you were a trooper through it all! Thank you for believing in me!

To my daughter~ Thank you for enduring the countless hours I spent writing this book. Your constant questions about what was going to happen next, were inspiring, because even I didn't know. I am giving you permission to read this book when you are 30! Ha Ha!

To Ari, Denise, Kristy, and Amy~ You girls are the best beta readers anyone could ask for! You supported my journey and spent endless hours reading and rereading. Your suggestions, critiques, and encouragement helped me in ways you'll never understand. Thank you for listening to my obsession day after day!

To Jill~ You've been a great friend! When I came to you about my cover designs in frustration, you immediately volunteered to help. Your graphic designs alleviated a ton of stress for me and helped to capture the essence of my books. Thank you for saving the day!

To my readers~ Thank you for supporting me in this journey. Please spread the word if you have enjoyed this book. Without you, writing would still be a dream.

# About the Author

Sabrina Wagner lives in Sterling Heights, Michigan. She writes sweet, sassy, sexy romance novels featuring alpha males and the strong women who challenge them. Her books include The Hearts Series and the spin-off, Forever Inked Novels.

Sabrina believes that true friends should be treasured, a woman's strength is forged by the fire of affliction, and that everyone deserves a happy ending. She enjoys spending time with her family, walking on the beach, worshiping the sun and of course, reading. Sabrina is a hopeless romantic and knows all too well that life is full of twists and turns, but the bumpy road is what leads to our true destination.

Want to know about my new releases and upcoming sales?

Stay connected on:

Facebook~
https://www.facebook.com/sabrinawagnerauthor

Twitter~
https://twitter.com/SWagnerauthor

Instagram~
https://www.instagram.com/sabrinawagnerauthor

I'd love to hear from you.
Visit my website to connect with me.

www.sabrinawagnerauthor.com

Made in the USA
Monee, IL
29 October 2021